THE GIRL AND THE CLOCKWORK CROSSFIRE

NIKKI McCORMACK

ISBN : 0-9983765-2-3
ISBN-13 : 978-0-9983765-2-3
First Edition 2017

Published by
Elysium Books
Bellevue, WA

This is a work of fiction. All
character s, names, places and
events are the product of the
author's imagination or are
used fictitiously.

Written by Nikki McCormack
(h tt p s ://n i k k i m c c o r m a c k . c o m /)
Edited by M Evan Matyas
(h tt p s ://c h i m e r a e d i t i n g . c o m /)
Cover Design by Mark Reid
(http : //www . a u t h o r p a c k a g e s . com/)
Interior Design by Brian C. Short

•

*To Kai, for your extraordinary partnership
and for helping me find my muse again.*

And to Neko, for being my Macak.

•

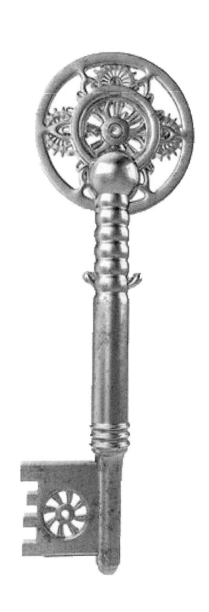

Officer Wells made it back to the London Juvenile and Adult Holding Facility a little after four in the morning. The first thing he had to take care of, after he sat behind his desk to start on the paperwork he needed to file, was the last thing he wanted to deal with after watching his new partner die.

Detective Emeraude stormed in through the front doors. She slapped a hand down on the front desk, glaring her frustration at him over the head of the officer on duty there. The man was a new recruit in spite of his advanced age. His flinch and anxious stare went unnoticed by the detective.

"There was a raid on a house in Chelsea last night. I need to know if anyone was taken or killed." The detective looked as miserable as Wells felt, with a heavily bandaged forearm and a scrape on her cheek.

Wells couldn't help but notice that the raw scrape on her cheek gave her typically harsh features a burst of color. He was not in the mood to deal with her or her impertinent demands.

"Detective Emeraude," Wells started, trying to keep it respectful, "I can't help you. I just lost a new recruit, and my superiors want me to clear it with them before I share any information with you."

Finding someone to help transport his late partner's

steamcycle and body back to JAHF had taken almost an hour with the rancid fog—fog so thick you could almost swim in it. The young officer was the latest in a string of short-lived new recruits. He was the latest, but he wasn't the first. The Literati's aggressive recruitment lately only added fuel to the fire, increasing the frequency and toll of confrontations with Pirate activists. It was getting too dangerous to venture out with an experienced team, let alone brave the streets with a trainee.

The situation made him miss his foul-tempered ex-partner Tagmet. Almost. Wells met Emeraude's gaze, making no effort to hide his miserable state. His head hurt. His heart, too. Another dead recruit.

"I've got a mountain of paperwork waiting," Wells said, hoping for some sympathy.

Emeraude didn't get the hint. She stared at him for a moment without comprehension, as though he'd spoken another language, then her expression darkened. "I need that information, Officer Wells. If you don't have it yet, you can get it. I'll wait." She took a few steps back, folded her arm across her chest and leaned against the wall.

Curious that she was demanding information on the same event the street rat had asked him about before scarpering off on the Pirate airship. Wells and the new recruit had been trying to apprehend the street rat and Asher, son of Captain Garrett. Captain Garrett would be happy that his son got away. Wells wasn't happy that a Pirate shot down his new recruit

Wells released a heavy breath, hoping some of his twitchy irritation would depart with the exhale. It didn't.

He shoved back from his desk, stood and walked around it to where she'd settled. Her stance shifted forward, pulling away from the wall as if poising for a possible attack. She was a bit taller than him, which made intimidation tactics difficult, but he'd had more than enough for one night.

"Maybe everyone else puts up with your attitude because they feel bad for you, but I didn't even work here when your brother died, so dredge up some bloody manners or get out." He pointed to the doors.

For an instant, something unexpected flickered across her features. A deep grief and guilt that made him feel a little sorry for even bringing her brother up despite his words. She held his gaze, the muscles in her jaw twitching, then she drew in a deep breath and the aggression in her stance faded a touch. She relaxed her arms.

Wells reciprocated, taking a step back out of her space.

"If there is any information at all that you can give me, I would appreciate it."

Her expression made it clear that the polite approach took considerable effort. To try to encourage that behavior, he turned to the desk officer who had actually been here to get a firsthand accounting of the raid. The man glanced between them uneasily. Wells nodded encouragement.

"There was a woman killed in the raid," the older man began. His eyes locked on Wells who gave another small nod to get him to continue. "And they brought in a young man who'd been injured. They said the others escaped in an older model airship. A real patchwork job."

Detective Emeraud leaned forward, eager. "Do you know who the woman was? Who's the youth they brought in?"

The other officer waited for Wells to nod once more before answering. "Don't know about the woman, but our records show that the youth has been through here several times. A street rat turned kidsman who goes by the name of Chaff."

Wells tuned in more intently then.

Chaff?

That was who the street rat asked him to check on. With the dead recruit to deal with, he hadn't even looked yet to see if anyone was brought in from the raid. Now he had that answer at least.

Em nodded once and spun on her heel, darting out the door without another word. The desk officer stared after her, looking puzzled. Wells shrugged. She'd been nicer than usual once he made it clear he wasn't in the mood for her abuse. Something to keep in mind for next time she came around. Although he would have liked to question her about her interest in the house raid before she rushed off.

He turned to the man at the desk. "You said this Chaff was brought in injured?"

The officer nodded. "Shot in the hand."

Wells winced. That would be a nasty wound. Lots of bones in a hand for a bullet to break. "Has a physician seen to it?"

"No, Sir. One of the officers wrapped it and said someone would be by later."

Far from satisfactory treatment. Wells tried to

ignore the uneasy swirl in his stomach. Even prisoners were supposed to receive appropriate medical care, which did at least give him the excuse he needed to investigate. He wasn't doing it for the street rat of course—he had gotten in enough trouble for aiding her during the search for Lucian Folesworth even though she had found the missing inventor—but for his own curiosity.

"I'll go check on him."

"Yes, Sir."

Wells strode down the hall, through the east intake room, and back into the east cellblock. The block was empty now aside from a passed out drunk in the first cell and the young man in the fourth. The youth sat on the cot with his head bowed and one hand, bloated with a crude wrapping of bandages, held high against his chest. His eyes squeezed shut and he wore a pained grimace. Bright blood seeped through the thick wraps. His pallor wasn't reassuring.

"Chaff?"

A slight tensing of his jaw was the only response. It was confirmation enough.

Why hadn't they seen to the injury more thoroughly?

"Have you had anything for the pain?"

"No," he answered hoarsely.

What was the street rat's interest in him? She might have been one of his thieves, though he didn't look that much older than her. "Are you a Pirate?"

"I may be daft," he rasped, "but I'm not a bloody Pirate."

He looked up then, his blue eyes red-rimmed and

glassy with pain. Sweat beaded on his brow beneath a mop of dusty blond hair.

He was a decent looking bloke. He might be almost handsome under different circumstances. Perhaps… "You know a young Asian girl? A creature of the streets like you?"

A flicker of panic chased away the grimace for a second. "Is she all right?"

That made things clearer. Whatever her interest in him, the youth obviously cared about her. "She got away. I don't know if that qualifies as all right considering the company she's keeping."

Chaff bowed his head again. He didn't say anything else.

Wells shifted his feet. He wanted to keep the conversation going, try to learn something about the situation, but the youth was in such obvious agony. It felt wrong to interrogate him.

Before he could think of something more to say, the door swung open and two men strode into the cellblock. The first was Joel Jacard, partner in Clockwork Enterprises. The other was a man called Bennett, a lean, fierce-looking chap Wells had seen with Lucian Folesworth. The latter didn't look like much more than a common thug. Given the way he hovered quietly behind whomever he was with and rarely spoke, Wells suspected Mr. Folesworth had hired him as a bodyguard.

But now Lucian Folesworth's brother was dead, and Bennett, for all his menacing presence, wasn't the one who inspired Wells to step away from the two of them. Wells didn't know much about Bennett, but he couldn't forget that Mr. Jacard had been on the inside of those bars, and his incarceration, however brief, had been full of hateful and vile threats toward the street rat—and Folesworth himself. Folesworth might have forgiven Joel and given him back his considerable rank and privilege. Wells couldn't shake the feeling of wrongness the man gave him.

Joel gave Wells a curt nod. "Good evening officer. We're here to see this new prisoner of yours."

Wells shifted his feet, fighting the urge to slink out like a mistreated dog and let them have the run of the place. "I'm not sure this is a good time. He needs medical attention."

Joel waved off his concern and walked up to the bars. "Rat, you want to tell me where your friends went."

"They're no mates of mine." Chaff's harsh, resentful tone was enough to convince Wells he might be sincere, though his interrogator appeared uninterested in the truth.

"Really?" Joel chuckled. "I find that hard to believe, but if it's true, then you won't mind telling me where they went."

"I'm not telling you anything."

Joel smiled pleasantly. "I can give you something for the pain."

A sick feeling spread through Wells, like poison racing through his blood. They should be giving the boy treatment regardless of his crimes, not using that care as a bribe.

Chaff slowly raised his head, his bloodshot eyes glaring purest hatred into Joel. "Bugger off. I'm not talking to you."

Joel's head tilted to one side and he narrowed his

eyes suspiciously at the youth.

"I know you," he said after a few seconds of scrutiny. "You were with that detective the night they arrested me."

The darker look vanished as quickly as it had appeared and Joel smiled again.

"It seems we've traded places." He leaned close to the bars, grinning like a merry demon now. "I promise to make sure you enjoy your stay."

Chaff dropped his head back against the wall with a groan. His eyes squeezed shut and he clutched the wrist of his injured hand. More blood stained the bandage now. Wells got the feeling the youth wasn't going to hear them anymore. His pain consumed him. Did he realize they would have to amputate it if it wasn't tended properly soon? It might be too late already.

Joel turned to Wells. "Someone will be here within the hour to move him to the new facility."

"The new place? He doesn't look that dangerous to me. Besides, moving him now is just going to make that hand worse."

Bennett smirked and Joel's lip twitched in a hint of a sneer. "Perhaps you would do well to remember that we're on the same side of the bars now and my authority comes from high above you."

Yes. They were on the same side of the bars now. Not long ago, Lucian Folesworth had been more than ready to see Joel die for his crimes. How could Lucian welcome the man back so enthusiastically? Perhaps the evidence proving Joel's innocence was truly irrefutable. Wells hadn't been part of that investigation, but he found when he tried to swallow the pill of Joel's exoneration, it stuck in his throat.

"Shouldn't we at least see to his hand before moving him?"

Joel glanced at Chaff and sneered. "He'll live. Let them deal with it there."

Wells watched them go, then turned to look at the youth in the cell again. It didn't sit well with him to leave a prisoner like that. Something about the whole situation didn't feel right. It made him want to go try to hunt down the girl, to tell her everything he knew about Chaff and where they were taking him. He'd spent his whole childhood dreaming of a life as an officer of the law. Upholding justice. Defending the weak. This wasn't justice and the idea that he was a part of it only made him feel sick.

He took hold of one of the bars. Perhaps he had gone barmy or perhaps he was just now coming to his senses. "Hang in there, mate. I'll tell her where they're taking you."

Chaff's eyes snapped open, his gaze feverish and intense. "No! Tell her nothing. Tell her you don't know where I am. Please."

Wells stepped back from that burning gaze, from the pain and the desperation. He shook his head and walked away. There was no doubt about it now. He hated his job.

Maeko hugged her arms around her, pulling Chaff's jacket tight to ward off the chill of the foggy night. The chill wasn't just from the cool evening. The offer Thaddeus had made her rang back in her mind. She would have to sell out all the Pirates at Drake's manor to save Chaff, but he had promised to leave them in peace if she did so. Most she didn't know. That didn't mean they deserved what the Literati would do to them if she betrayed their location. And her mum and Ash were there now.

What did it say about her that she still considered it a legitimate offer?

A soft hissing sound above her drew her attention. Peering up, she saw a shape dropping down from the darkness. It was an airship much like the sleek compact model that had exploded over the Airship Tower with Lucian Folesworth in it the night his twin brother Thaddeus took his place, only this one was painted a flat black. It almost vanished in the night. A door opened in the side of the small gondola and a rope ladder dropped down. She grabbed hold of the bottom rung. The ship began to rise again while she climbed, the engines so quiet it was hard to tell they were operational. When she got to the top, Drake grabbed her arm and pulled her in.

"Bring up the ladder if you would." He shut the door and returned to the captain's seat.

"Where's Crimson?"

"She rode back in the coach," he answered, his attention focused on making a few adjustments in their course.

She began to pull in the ladder, rolling it neatly into the storage hatch in the floor. "Is this ship the other delivery you were talking about?"

"Yes. Isn't she beautiful?" He ran his fingers across the control panel with a gentleness typically reserved for infants or lovers.

"It's black?"

"A custom order."

"And quiet."

He grinned back at her, the expression not quite as feral looking now that he'd shaved. In fact, there was something oddly childlike in the expression. "That is the best part. I bought her so I could study the engines. If I can make my battleship half this quiet, we'll be able to get in close to start firing on our target before they even know we're there. Did you find the crates?"

"Yes. They're in the building. I overheard them saying they were going to move them out to the new facility sometime later in the week."

"Good work. Did you run into any trouble?"

"No." She didn't want to lie to him, but they hadn't discussed her price yet. One should always keep their options open.

"I told you it would be simple." He stood up and gestured to the chair. "Want to fly her?"

Wary of the sudden snap of excitement his offer

triggered in her, she stepped back. "I can't. I don't know how."

"It's easy. Have a seat and I'll show you."

She sat and stared at the unfamiliar controls, a sparkle of mixed anticipation and anxiety lighting her nerves on fire.

Drake chuckled. He was in a bright mood with the acquisition of this new toy. "They won't bite you."

He leaned close behind her in a manner that would have made her uneasy with most anyone else. Somehow, with him, the nearness didn't have that sense of impropriety. Perhaps because she knew he was in a relationship with Crimson or because his childlike enthusiasm over the machine made him somehow less threatening.

He gave her a quick explanation of all the controls then stepped back and began fiddling with an odd little contraption he pulled out of one pocket.

He was right. It was easy. She gave it a little more power and steered to the right. It began a graceful arc in that direction.

"Feel that. She's more responsive than a good horse."

Maeko grinned and swept it gracefully back the other way. She'd never ridden a horse, so she would have to take his word on that part. It gave her a heady sense of freedom and power, being able to control the flying machine.

He sat back and watched with his pleased grin, letting her fly for a while, taking them in a random course off through the nighttime countryside. Eventually, he took back the controls and steered them toward the estate again.

The device he'd been fiddling with slipped back into one pocket.

"What's that?"

His smile was full of mystery. "A key of sorts. Maybe I'll show it to you some day."

It was clear from his look that flying the airship was the extent of his generosity at the moment. It was more than she had expected. She curled in one of the plush chairs and dozed until she heard the soft hiss of air being drawn in.

She opened her eyes. Early morning light had begun to peek over the horizon. Below them, the roof of one of the big outbuildings had opened and they were sinking down into it. They sank deep, into what turned out to be the huge underground hangar where the battleship and several smaller ships were under construction. It only took two men to help bring the small ship down. The roof closed in over them.

"What next?"

Drake walked over to open the door of the gondola. "We go after that shipment before it gets moved. We'll give things a little time to cool down, then I'll help you get in touch with your Literati contact."

He stepped out of the ship.

Maeko hesitated a moment then hurried after him. She fell into step with him, heading up and out of the underground workshop. "Before I agree to help you any more…"

He glanced over at her and, to her surprise, he looked rather pleased. "You have your own agenda. I can appreciate that. If you're interested in joining me for breakfast, we could discuss it more."

"I…" Had he really just asked her to eat with him? "Um. Yes, I suppose. Thank you."

With nothing else to say, she followed him out through the door only to find Ash and her mother waiting in the massive foyer. They descended on her like a pair of vultures on fresh meat.

Tomoe grabbed her shoulders. "Where did you go? I woke up and you were gone." She gave Drake a fierce glare to which he returned a cheerful smile.

Maeko shrugged off her hands and stepped back. "I was only helping with an errand. It wasn't a big deal."

"And I dare say she quite enjoyed flying the new airship," Drake interjected.

A smile slipped out before she could stop it.

Ash glared daggers into Drake.

"It was rather fun," she admitted.

"Breakfast should already be served in the formal dining room for whoever is interested. It would be a shame for any of you to miss out on Miss Denson's delightful cooking," Drake offered.

Ash and Tomoe exchanged looks, then Ash turned to Maeko. "You hungry?"

A twinge of guilt turned her gut. Her gaze flickered to Drake.

He took that for the prompt it was. "Maeko will be dining with me this morning. There are things we need to discuss. I'm sure she'd be pleased to join you later."

The daggers Ash glared into Drake were now poison coated. He met her eyes. "Mae?"

"We'll talk later. I promise."

Drake turned and walked away then. She followed,

leaving Ash staring forlornly after her. That she was wearing Chaff's jacket certainly wasn't going to help the situation. They needed to have a long talk, but the sad truth was, she didn't know what to say. What did she feel for him? For Chaff? Without knowing those answers, what could she really say to him? All she knew was that she had to help Chaff and he needed to help his father. That was their purpose for now. Everything else would have to wait.

Drake led her to a small private dining room that included an elegant sitting area. The back wall of the room was lined with large windows overlooking the rear horse pastures. Two fine silver place settings were laid out on a small table with several covered silver serving platters sitting in the center.

She looked askance at him.

He shrugged. "I had already planned to invite you to eat with me today. You have considerable potential that I would love to see used to our benefit, but I would have to be blind not to see your reluctance. There is something holding you back. If we are going to be of any use to one another, that needs to come out in the open." He pulled out one chair for her and politely waited for her to sit.

Thaddeus's offer played back in her mind. On the surface, a quick and easy way to get what she wanted, but only if she was willing to sacrifice a number of lives to get it.

Maeko sat and let him slide the chair in for her. "I want your help getting Chaff away from the Literati. Give me that and I will do whatever I can to help you."

He gave her a guarded look and took his seat.

"Chaff? He's the young man who warned us of the Lits approach at Tomoe's house? The one that got shot in the hand?"

"Yes."

A woman entered the room and silently began to pull the covers off the platters. Savory aromas rose from the dishes and Maeko's mouth began to water in response.

"That's your price?" Drake asked, not looking at her.

"It is."

"That will require a more cautious approach than I had planned, but, if I am to be honest, I would like to get Garrett back as well. I believe you can help with that. I promise you that, if we can find him, I will do everything in my power to extract him from Lit custody if it can be done safely…"

He trailed off when she began to shake her head.

"Not good enough. I will find him. I will do whatever you need me to after you help me free him."

The woman served up a portion of roast pheasant to each of them. It smelled delicious. Drake took a bite and chewed slowly. Maeko refused to look at her plate as she waited for his answer. Her stomach betrayed her with a loud grumble.

Drake swallowed and washed it down with a sip of the wine that had been poured for them, then he met her eyes. "I promise I will help you find and free your Chaff."

She held his gaze steadily. "Then I promise I will help you fight the Literati."

Drake smiled and lifted his glass. "To seal the deal."

She lifted her glass and they toasted the agreement. No one else would approve. Not even Chaff, she was willing to bet. It didn't matter. The deal had been made.

Now to address another problem. "Why do you dislike Ash so much?"

Drake turned his attention to cutting away another bite of the pheasant.

This time she followed his example.

"I don't dislike him. He's a good lad. Like his father, he isn't willing to see the people he cares about get hurt. He's not cut out for this and it is my intent to discourage him from getting involved."

Did that mean he thought she was willing to see the people she cared about get hurt? Maybe he was right about that. After all, hadn't she led Chaff into this?

She pushed the thought away. "So you're trying to discourage him to protect him?"

"Yes. His father was one of those Pirates I met when I ran away. He is a good friend. I would no more hurt his son than I would him. I only hope that your contact can help us find him as well as your friend."

Maeko turned her attention to the savory dishes for a time. When she'd eaten enough to take the edge off her hunger, she asked another question itching at her mind. "Doesn't Crimson eat with you?"

His fond smile spoke volumes to that relationship. It almost made him look like a more docile wolf. "I've seen little of her since we brought the drawings you stole from Mr. Folesworth. She's spent most every waking moment working with those designs."

"So, you two aren't married?"

His dark eyes focused through the windows. "No.

For all that I've never gotten along with my peers, my family name still makes me an eligible bachelor. I do have to put in social appearances on occasion. When people ask awkward questions about how I spend my time, I can often distract them by asking about their daughters. One must keep up a good front in my position. Marrying below my station would draw unwanted attention and deny me an easy out at social gatherings."

"And if they don't have an eligible daughter?"

"Then I mention the newest promising stallion in my stables. My family has always been renowned for raising some of the finest horses."

She took the last bite of pheasant from her plate, chewing it slowly to savor the tender meat. It almost melted in her mouth. The more she learned about Drake, the less uneasy he made her, but something about him still bothered her. It might be nothing more than his wealth. The fact that he chose to risk all of the comforts he enjoyed on this made very little sense to her.

"They'll expect you to marry eventually, won't they?"

"I can string them along a little longer." He cut away another serving of the pheasant and put it on her plate.

"I shouldn't."

"Why?" He gave her a quick appraising look. "I don't think it's going to damage your figure. You're narrow as a lamppost. A little meat on your bones and you'd be a lovely image in a dress."

She shrugged off the compliment awkwardly and began to cut away a bite of the pheasant. "I don't really like dresses."

"I'm not surprised. You're a lot like Crimson that way."

"But she would look stunning in a dress."

Drake nodded agreement. "I'll tell her you said so."

"What do we do next?"

Drake slid his plate away and sat back in his chair. "You will need to get in touch with your Lit contact as soon we can get you safely into the city and I need to work on the problem of getting my supplies back. I've got contacts in the city keeping an eye on things. I'll let them know who you're trying to get in touch with. They'll scout things out and figure out the best time to get you into the city. I imagine you'll want to catch up on sleep today."

She nodded. She was tired, more so now that her stomach was full of rich foods, but she didn't want to wait much longer. Who knew what might happen to Chaff if she didn't get him back quickly.

C H A P T E R   T H R E E

Maeko leaned back against the wall, watching Ash work industriously on the slowly forming shape of Drake's airship. He hadn't noticed her. His pale green eyes were bright with intense focus. Sweat beaded on his forehead. There was something in his expression, something that broke through the grim determination to rescue his father, Captain Garrett. It was a hint of satisfaction. He loved this work. It was the kind of work Maeko knew he'd done with his father before the Literati took Garrett away. That satisfaction told her that she'd at least made the right choice in telling Drake that Ash could help with the airship.

The head mechanic, a muscular chap with a cropped head of dusty-blond hair, was also watching Ash. After a moment, he glanced her way, gave a nod and a wink and went back to his work.

Farther back in the underground hanger sat Drake's new personal airship, already dwarfed by the fast-growing battleship.

Worry festered like a slow disease in her chest.

Over a week had passed since Thaddeus made his offer. His thug, Bennett, would be on orders to kill her if he saw her now. She'd passed up one offer. What was happening to Chaff while she waited for Drake to come through?

20

She rubbed her arms, gooseflesh rising on them in memory of the chill on the rooftop of the warehouse that night. Of her encounter with Thaddeus and Bennett, whose skill at stealth had made her feel like a bumbling amateur when he caught her sneaking around the crates.

A yowl snapped her back to the present.

Maeko turned and strode over to the table Macak was standing on, the panel of his clockwork leg hanging open and his ears half-back as he turned angry kitty eyes on one of the men around the table. All three men stepped back, looking guilty. She pinned each of them with a look of warning.

"If you can't treat him well, you don't get to study his leg." She gave him an icy look.

"Sorry Miss," a burly bloke said. He wore a monocle with a variety of attachments that poked out in every direction. He cleared his throat and a hint of pink rose in his cheeks. "I slipped."

She glanced at the glove he wore, also laden with a plethora of integrated tools, some of which looked like instruments of torture. "Where's Crimson?"

As if waiting for her cue, the woman sashayed into the room, bright red hair giving advance warning of her fiery personality. A soft green bodice and jewel-toned waistcoat gave her an elegant femininity that her trousers somehow didn't detract from. Her green eyes swept the scene, and she walked up to the table, closing the panel on Macak's leg and flipping the latch with one bright red nail. Macak leapt up to Maeko's shoulders, still staring feline fury at the man with the monocle.

"Looks like it's time for a break," Crimson

observed. "Mae, darling, why don't you head up and take a bit of a nap. It's going to be a late night."

Maeko's skipped a beat. With that one phrase, she felt as though someone had woken her from a stupor. It was almost time to start working on Chaff and Garrett's freedom. "Is it time?"

Crimson nodded. "I'll come get you later when we're ready to leave."

Reacting to her sudden excitement and anxiety, Macak head-butted her cheek with jarring enthusiasm. She scratched his head and nodded to Crimson. "I'll be ready."

With more purpose in her strides now, she went straight to the room she shared with her mother with its ornate scrollwork and elegant painted ceiling, happy to find it empty. She crawled into the big soft canopy bed, determined to be rested for the evening foray into the city. Anticipation and uncertainty fought the lulling effect of Macak's warmth and rhythmic purring. The cat eventually won.

#

"Maeko."

That wasn't Crimson.

She opened her eyes, stretched and, in spite of how much she dreaded the idea of talking to Ash right then, a small smile curved her lips. For the first time since leaving the flat at the Airship Tower the night she and Chaff stole Lucian's blueprints, she felt rested. Her back and neck didn't hurt as badly as they had, probably thanks to a proper bed. The bruises from the attack that caused those injuries had almost healed enough for her to lie on her back again.

If not for Chaff and Diggs, that attack would have been fatal.

The smile faded a little.

"Well, you're not scowling at me. I'll take that as a good sign."

"Why would I scowl at you?" She held onto the smile, finding it not as hard to do so as she might have expected. In a way, it was good to see Ash without anyone else around to add to the tension. "Other than the fact that your presence in my bedroom would be considered improper by just about anyone else in the building."

He shrugged and muttered, "No one saw me come in."

She gave him a teasing wink. "Oh, that makes it all right then. Perhaps if you said you only came in to help me get dressed…"

Ash flushed and she giggled.

"I suppose I should leave."

She snaked a hand out of the covers and grabbed his wrist when he turned to go. He looked at her hand in surprise and met her eyes. His gaze dropped away again.

"Just toss me those clothes." She released his wrist and pointed to a pile on the vanity.

Ash got the clothes and handed them to her.

"Turn around."

He did as ordered and she squirmed into her clothes without getting out from under the covers. The ability to change quickly and discreetly in almost any setting was a necessary skill when you lived most of your life in hideouts surrounded by a bunch of boys. When she was done, she threw off the blankets, burying Macak on the bed behind her. The cat made a small sound of protest though he didn't wake up enough to dig himself free. She tapped Ash on the shoulder and he turned, automatically glancing down to confirm that she was indeed properly clothed.

His flush brightened a bit more. "I didn't mean to wake you, it's just that—"

"Yes, you did. What's on your mind?" That was a dangerous question. Still, she couldn't avoid him forever and didn't really want to now that she thought about it with a clearer head. She sat cross-legged on the bed and gestured for him to join her. He sat on the edge of the bed, his posture upright and tense.

"Where did you go that night? The first night we were here."

She hated to lie to him. The truth would only upset him though, and she didn't intend to tell anyone about her encounter with Thaddeus. The offer was technically expired, but she suspected he would still go along with it if she went to him with information on the Pirate hideout. "Drake wanted to talk so he invited me along to pick up his new airship."

"And he wanted to keep talking over breakfast?"

She pulled the covers off Macak and scratched his head, avoiding Ash's gaze. "Yes."

"Since you two are new best mates, you must know what he's planning to do with that battleship we're building?"

An innocent enough question really, though one she would have to answer cautiously. "It isn't like that, he just thinks I have skills and connections that might be of use. Right now, he's trying to get his hands on more supplies for the projects he's working on to fight the Lits and he's also looking for a way to get your dad back."

Ash looked shocked by that. "Is he?"

She shoved him playfully when he scowled, fishing for a lighter mood to ease the weight that seemed to be smothering him. "Yes. He isn't as bad as you think he is."

Ash responded with a faint, dubious smile. "What does he want you to do?"

"I'm going to go find out where Garrett and Chaff are being held. Which I would be doing with or without him wanting me to," she added when he frowned.

"But he does want you to do it?"

Her smile was losing its staying power. "Yes."

"Drake may not care what happens to you, but I'm worried you're going to get hurt."

She thought of Bennett with his scarred nose and baby blue eyes. It took considerable self-control to hold back a shudder. If she only got hurt, she'd count herself lucky. "I'm going to be careful, but I can get the information we need. Would you rather we left your dad in Literati hands?"

He hung his head and the muscles in his jaw jumped. Maeko knew he didn't like choosing between her safety and his father's freedom. That was rather sweet really and perhaps it was somewhat mean of her to put him in that spot. Still, nothing would change the truth and he needed to make his peace with that.

"No," he admitted hesitantly, as if the very words hurt coming out. "But why does it always have to be you?"

She touched his arm and his gaze moved to her hand. "I'm not the only one out there taking risks, Ash, I'm just the only one you notice. I have my own goals, and right now they happen to coincide with some of the things Drake is after." She left it there. At this point, either he would understand that or he wouldn't.

He chewed at his lip for a moment, and she waited. He met her eyes, then glanced away again. "Can I at least do something to help?"

"This next part I need to do alone. After that... maybe."

He nodded as if he had expected the answer and stared at his hands in his lap. After a brief silence, he made himself look at her with a visible force of will. "What happened after you came to warn me the night Lucian was murdered?"

"I went to one of the hideouts by Cheapside like I said I was going to, and some nasty bloke tried to kill me. Diggs and Chaff stopped him." She remembered the dog the man had tortured and did shudder this time. Did it bother Diggs that he had shot and killed that man? Did it bother her? "They took care of me after that."

"And?"

Her fading smile failed completely then. "And what?"

"What about you and Chaff?"

She got up from the bed and walked over to the vanity. Her hands came to rest on the back of the chair there, where Chaff's jacket hung. She saw him in her mind, falling from the airship ladder after the Lits shot him in the hand, the pain etched in his face. Sorrow stabbed into her like a blade, twisting in her chest. Anger and frustration blazed white behind her vision. Her hands tightened on the jacket.

"What exactly do you want me to say? Do you want a minute-by-minute account? Are you just looking for a reason to be jealous? Do you want to hear that he kissed me? Is that what you're after? Would it satisfy you to know that I rather liked it?"

She snapped her mouth shut. What was she doing? She closed her eyes and tried to find a calm within herself. She couldn't look at Ash in the mirror's reflection and see the hurt in his face, the hurt she caused him. Tears stung at the corners of her eyes. She wanted so badly to fix everything, but all she could do was make a bigger mess of it.

"I'm sorry, Mae."

He was right behind her now. His hands came to rest on her shoulders. When she didn't respond, he used gentle force to turn her around. She couldn't bring herself look at him.

"I didn't mean to upset you, but I am jealous. I can't help it. He got to be with you when you needed someone the most."

Was he suggesting that the result would have been the same had he been the one to save her and take care of her instead of Chaff? Was he wrong? She drew in a breath, trying to swallow down the urge to cry and find her calm again. After a moment, she opened her eyes and he smiled, a gentle, hopeful expression.

His hand came up to cup her cheek. "But I'm here for you now."

She closed her eyes again quickly. Confusion,

frustration, and a selfish longing to accept his comfort swept a tempest through her. It would be easy to give in to his affections, to let him hold and comfort her. But what would happen when she got Chaff back? Who would she turn away? She couldn't have them both. Not like that.

She swallowed. Her throat felt too tight. She had to force the words out. "Please, don't."

He pulled away abruptly and she opened her eyes to see his back as he stormed from the room. The door slammed shut behind him and opened again almost immediately. Crimson entered, glancing over her shoulder once after Ash.

She looked askance at Maeko. "Lover's spat?"

"We're not…" Maeko shook her head. "Never mind."

"Oh." She smiled knowingly. "That explains a lot. He wants to be and you're smitten with that other boy, the one Drake told me about." She snapped her fingers. "What was his name?"

"Chaff," Maeko grumbled. "And I'm not smitten with him."

Crimson shrugged. "I've got to run into town for some things. Drake told me to ride in with you. I can do my errands while you meet up with your contact. Our scouts in the city said he spends an occasional evening at JAHF, but has been spending most of his evenings on patrol in the Whitechapel area, so we'll try that."

"Finally," Maeko muttered. She turned back to the vanity and Chaff's jacket, resting her hand on it for a moment.

"Which of the boys you're not smitten with does

that belong to?"

Maeko gave her a hard look.

Crimson laughed. It sounded like chimes ringing in a light breeze.

"I'm only teasing you, Kitten. Your affairs are your own business." She turned toward the door, beckoning Maeko with one red nailed finger. Then she paused and looked over her shoulder. "Unless you'd like to talk about it."

Maeko considered the offer for a few seconds. It might be nice to get the whole mess off her chest. It might even help her figure out how she really felt. Then again, that thought worried her almost more than the current confusion. At least while she remained uncertain she didn't have to figure out how to admit her preference for one to the other.

She shook her head.

"Come along then."

"Wait."

Crimson raised her brows in question.

"I think I should dress a bit differently if I'm going to approach this particular contact without drawing the wrong attention. Can you help me?"

Crimson shut the door and Maeko pulled out the dress she'd worn the night she ran from the Airship Tower. The only one she still had of the several finely made ones Lucian gave to her while she lived with him. She'd had one of Drake's servants clean and hang it in case she had a need for it. Approaching a Literati officer might be easier if she looked like an upstanding citizen when she did it. At the very least, she suspected it would put Wells more at ease with her.

Once dressed, Maeko followed Crimson through the manor, hoping to slip out unseen in the fine togs. That hope was dashed the moment they stepped outside. Ash stood off by of the stables talking with Tomoe and his little brother, when she and Crimson walked out into the courtyard.

A coach waited out in front of the house with two fine matched black horses standing patient in the traces. Tomoe and Ash looked like they had a mind to intervene when they saw her, so she kept her eyes ahead, pretending not to see them, and hurried straight to the coach.

Crimson wasted no time stepping into the coach and getting settled. Had she also noticed the potential for confrontation or did she just do everything with such haste?

Maeko stepped in immediately after her. When the door closed behind them and the coach began to move, she breathed a sigh of relief.

"I have to admit," Crimson began, "Ash seems like a nice boy and he is handsome, especially with those pretty pale eyes. Why does his attention bother you so much? A bird in the hand, as they say."

Maeko leaned against the side of the coach and peered out the window to watch the long pasture fence line as they passed by. Part of her resented that Crimson was pursuing the subject, but another larger part was heartened by the idea of having someone to talk to about it. "It isn't that I don't like Ash. I do. He just doesn't understand me."

Crimson crossed her long legs on the seat and set her hands in her lap, her bright green eyes boring into Maeko with a gentle and relentless pressure. "In what way?"

"He doesn't understand what it's like to live on the streets. He seems to think being a street rat is some kind of vice I should overcome, like an opium addiction. Life on the streets is rubbish. Lots of sickness, hunger, and running from the Lits, but at least I never had to pretend to be something I'm not and I had people who cared about me. People who would watch my back if I needed it. From what I've seen, all this proper rubbish means is that you're expected to conform to the expectations of other people who would happily stab you in the back if they thought it would gain them a little more status to flaunt."

"It certainly can be that way sometimes." Crimson's smile was gentle, full of understanding and a gleam of mischief. "Maybe even most of the time. I take it you feel like this Chaff does understand you?"

"He was my mentor. He protected me and taught me how to get by living on the streets. He knows who and what I am and accepts that, though I imagine he'd be chuffed as anyone if I stopped taking so many risks." She exhaled, trying to relieve the sudden tightening in her chest. "He wouldn't be in this mess if not for me."

Crimson's eyes shone in the dimness of the coach

like two gemstones. Even with her somewhat hooked
nose, she was a stunning woman.

"I've been wondering about that. How *did* you get
involved in all of this?"

"Macak."

Crimson's brow crinkled in confusion.

"I found him in an alley when I was hiding from the
Lits. I decided to take care of him. With his clockwork
leg, he wasn't safe roaming the streets. One thing led to
another in a rather whirlwind sort of way and I ended
up helping Lucian survive the plotting of his homicidal
partner. A lot of good all that did." It irked to think how
much she had risked with nothing to show for it now.
"Lucian took me in after I saved him. Then his brother
murdered him and took his place. So here I am, still
trying to help the people I care about and mostly
making things worse."

Crimson leaned forward and took one of Maeko's
hands in hers. "You can't blame yourself, Kitten.
Things happen. You try harder than most people I know
to get things right. How many people would truly risk
their own life to save someone else? You should be
proud of your courage."

"They shot Chaff. Should I be proud of that?" Her
voice caught and she looked away to hide the tears
welling in her eyes.

Crimson moved gracefully into the seat next to her,
unaffected by the rocking and bouncing of the coach,
and put an arm around her. Maeko tried to fight the
tears, but she'd grown weary of holding it in. She let
the woman pull her close and stroke her hair while she
let some of the tears go.

"Don't fret, Kitten. Drake gave his word that he'd help get Chaff free and I'll see to it that he follows through."

"Thank you."

Maeko moved to wipe her nose on her sleeve and Crimson caught her wrist. She dug a handkerchief out of a trouser pocket with her other hand. "Please don't do that to such a lovely dress."

Maeko flushed and accepted the handkerchief.

#

Dusk was settling on the city by the time the coach dropped Maeko off in Whitechapel not far from the lurk where Wells and the other officer had begun tailing them the night after Chaff was taken. It wasn't raining, which meant there were a fair number of people about for her to blend in with. Unfortunately, the fact that she was better dressed than over half the people on the streets left her feeling awkward and ill at ease. Ordinarily, a young lady of obvious wealth wouldn't be wandering the Whitechapel streets without a chaperone. Perhaps she should have asked for someone to come with her, but instead she had insisted on going alone thinking Wells might be more comfortable without someone else there. She forced her shoulders back and her chin up, keeping a steady stride to discourage those who gave her a second look from following up on their curiosity.

How did one find a Literati officer patrolling the streets? It wasn't as if she went looking for them often. She knew far more about hiding from them than she did about how to approach one. Then again, knowing how to avoid the officers should be a simple reverse of how to find them.

Using that theory, it wasn't long before she spotted a couple of Literati officers chatting up a gentleman while he was locking up his storefront. Neither was Wells, though they were both as young or younger than him. They laughed at something the shop owner said and bid him a jovial farewell then started down the street in her direction. Fighting the instinct to duck down an alley, she continued toward them and smiled politely when they were only a few strides away.

"Excuse me, officers." Her voice shook a little.

The two men stopped and regarded her with a hint of surprise.

The one on the right, a young man with a long pointed nose that poked down well over his neat brown moustache, offered a friendly smile. When he spoke, he had a slightly nasal voice. "How can we assist you, Miss?"

She drew in a small breath to steady her nerves. *Remember, Mae, you're a lady right now.* "I'm looking for Officer Wells. Is he around?"

The other officer, a pale chap with icy blue eyes and white-blond hair grinned. "I didn't know he liked them so young."

Maeko's first impulse was to punch the bloke, but she had a feeling that fell under the category of things a proper young lady didn't do. Instead, she gasped and put her fingers over her lips in what she hoped was a convincingly feminine display of shock.

The first officer elbowed his partner sharply in the ribs, sending the other staggering to one side, his face turning an unflattering shade of pink.

"Pardon him, Miss. His parents didn't teach him any manners. Wells would normally be here, but he's been put on light duty. He suffered an injury when he and his partner were attacked by Pirates few nights ago."

Light duty? What did that mean? She ignored the rude officer and gave the nicer officer a concerned look. "I do hope he's all right."

"He should be fine, Miss. He's back working in the office at JAHF for the remainder of the week while he heals up."

The blond officer stepped back up beside his partner, looking sullen and rubbing his side. "I'm sure he'd welcome a visit. Desk duty is bloody dull."

"What kind of language is that to be using in front of a lady?"

The blond flinched away from the threat of another elbow in the ribs.

"Sorry, Miss," he apologized.

She nodded curtly at the blond, remembering to be incensed by language she used more often than not herself, then smiled at the first man. "Thank you for your assistance."

He inclined his head politely. "Anytime, Miss."

Maeko continued down the street, waiting until the two officers were out of sight to hail a hansom. She felt calmer settled in the seat with Whitechapel fading behind her, at least until she considered where she was headed. It might be nothing short of madness to go to JAHF when she'd escaped from the place twice in the recent past. Without knowing where Wells lived, however, it was the only way she was likely to catch him. She chewed at the nub of a fingernail all the way

over. When the hansom pulled up in front of the
building, she stayed in the seat for a moment, reluctant
to set foot on the steps.

What's wrong with me? I can't go in there.

"This is the place, Miss," the coachman prompted.

"Yes. Thank you." She made herself step down
from the hansom. A sickly coiling sensation began in
her stomach as she paid the man and started walking up
the steps. Maybe she'd get lucky and Chaff would still
be there in one of the holding cells. It didn't seem likely,
but even the remotest chance was enough to keep her
walking to the doors.

The front door was locked so she rapped lightly on
it. She heard a chair scraping on the floor as someone
stood up inside. The lock clicked and an elderly
gentleman in a Literati uniform looked out and smiled,
displaying a rather prominent gap in his upper teeth.

"What do you need, Miss?"

"I'm sorry to bother you. I had hoped to speak with
Officer Wells. Is he here?"

The man looked her over, though she wondered
how well he saw her with his cloudy eyes. After a long
moment in which he stood staring through her with
pursed lips, he nodded. "Come in."

He shuffled back into the room and she followed,
doing her best not to jump visibly when the door
thudded shut behind her. Wells sat at one of the two
desks in the room looking over some papers. When he
looked up, he dropped the pen he was holding. He knew
who she was. A street rat playing at being a society lady.
After staring in open-mouthed surprise for a few
seconds, he closed his mouth and stood up.

"Miss…" Wells trailed off, raising a brow in question.

"Harris," she answered, then felt guilty for taking Ash's last name. Did Chaff even know his last name? She didn't remember ever asking.

He smiled tightly.

"Ah, yes. I have that information you wanted. If you would accompany me to the back office." At that, he walked to the double doors that led back into the rest of the building and opened one, gesturing for her to precede him through.

She hesitated before the doorway. Could she actually trust him? The further she went into the depths of this building, the harder it would be to get away if he meant to try to arrest her—and it wasn't as if he didn't have reason to do so.

"Don't worry, Miss Harris, an upstanding lady like you has nothing to fear back there." The slight grimace told her he knew it was a lie and he felt a smidge guilty for saying it.

She gave him a hard look then took a deep breath and walked past him into the bowels of the jail. He let the door shut and walked past her to lead the way down the hall at a brisk pace, challenging her skill in the heeled boots. She followed past the side halls that led to the two cellblocks, to another door near the end of the hall. He opened it and stepped aside to let her pass.

It led into an office with large comfortable chairs on either side of a heavy, polished wood desk. Tall filing cabinets lined the back wall, and a well-stocked liquor cabinet stood to one side with a crystal decanter full of some amber liquid on top.

Wells shut the door behind them.

When he finally turned and faced her, he shook his head and chuckled. "I don't know if you're the bravest girl I've ever met or the daftest. What are you thinking walking in here like this?"

He gestured to her outfit.

"You think the street rat look would've worked better?"

"No, but… I don't think you should be coming here dressed in any way."

"I'm certainly not coming here in my birthday suit."

"I didn't mean…" He flushed bright. "Just have a seat. Please," he added as walked around the desk and sank heavily into the chair. He had a run of stitches in an angry cut on his hand that made her think of Chaff and his injured hand.

Worry made her legs feel weak. She sat slowly, afraid to get too comfortable, but not sure she could stand steady in that moment.

"I should be locking you up, not giving you sensitive information."

She tensed, gripping the chair arms.

"Don't worry. I'm not planning on it. However, I'd be a sight more comfortable if I knew your proper name at least. I think we've come that far in our odd relationship."

"Maeko."

He actually smiled then and she shifted in her seat. Something about a Literati officer smiling at her made her distinctly uneasy.

"Not Maeko Harris, I'm betting."

She said nothing.

"Good enough. I'm afraid the news about your friend isn't good. They took him…" He trailed off, staring at the top of the desk.

She shifted to the edge of her seat. "What? Where did they take him?"

"You know, he begged me not to tell you, and after you had the audacity to walk in here, I think I can understand why. Still, I don't suppose it matters much. You can't do anything for him."

The air had escaped her lungs, finding no return route with the corset and leaving her with a faintly panicky shortness of breath. "You have to tell me."

"They took him to the new prison facility outside of the city."

"Is Garrett Harris there too?"

Recognition lit his eyes. "I thought Harris sounded familiar. Yes, he is, but you'll never get them out of there."

"I have to."

He sat forward, leaning his elbows on the desk and gave her a slow sympathetic shake of his head. "I'm sorry. There's no way you'll get into that place. You'd never get past the outer wall, let alone find the right building before they arrested or shot you."

She chewed at her lip and closed her eyes, struggling against a heavy weight that pressed down on her chest. It couldn't end this way.

She opened her eyes and Wells sat back away from her, resistance already building in his eyes.

"I could do it if you help me," Maeko said.

"No. I've already told you more than I should have."

"I can get past the outer wall if I go at night. I just

need you to tell me what building he's in."

"You don't listen too well." He reclined in the chair, the resistance in his bearing almost equal to the determination in hers. "I said no. Even if you got to the right building, the place is crawling with guards."

"Please. I have to try." She twisted her hands together in her lap to resist the desire to start chewing at a nail.

He was beginning to look distraught, perhaps unintentionally mirroring her distress. "Even if I wanted to, I couldn't help you. I don't know what building they're keeping him in."

She gave him that special pleading look that so often got her what she wanted. "You could find out. And you could find out when the shifts change. I just need a little more information."

Wells shook his head and clenched his jaw. He stood up and walked to the door, grabbing the handle.

"I'm an officer of the Literati. I can't help you with this." He opened the door and gestured for her to leave.

Her throat tightened. *I will not cry.* As she stood up, one traitorous tear slipped free. She lowered her gaze, wiping it away with a fierce swipe of her hand.

Wells slammed the door shut again. "Bloody birds and their bloody tears!"

That sounded promising. She looked up hopefully, letting another tear go free.

"Meet me back here in two nights. *If* I can find anything out, I'll tell you. But I'm not promising anything." He opened the door again and swept a hand in front of himself to usher her out.

Maeko grinned. On the way past, she popped up on

her toes and planted a quick kiss on his cheek.

"Don't be doing that." He followed her out, speaking a low voice. "If anyone saw that, do you know what they'd say?"

The blond officer in Whitechapel came to mind and she nodded. The perfect cover. "I suspect they may say those things anyway. Besides, you liked it."

Wells escorted her down the hall muttering something about birds under his breath.

The hour was getting late. Full dark entombed the city and Maeko was already at least a half hour late when she made it back to the rendezvous in Whitechapel. Crimson wasn't there, which raised the question of whether she had come and gone already or simply hadn't arrived yet. A couple shady-looking blokes stood on the corner. One wore a tattered waistcoat that was a few sizes too big. The other wore a shirt tucked in on one side and mismatched boots. Both had hair and beards in desperate need of a wash and trim, even by the standards of a street rat. It made sense to find a place to hole up out of sight nearby rather than linger in the open with such types around. The city felt more hostile than she liked. Passers-by looked long at her, their gazes heavy. The weight of being noticed made everything around her feel too close.

It had a good deal to do with the way she was dressed as much as any real change in the city, she suspected. Then again, with the rising tension between the Lits and the Pirates, the danger could also be very real.

Maeko changed directions to move away from the two shady blokes, but not before she felt their eyes on her.

"Hey, poppet, where you going?" One nudged the

other, and they broke into a trot to cross the street.

She hadn't thought to bring any kind of weapon, dressed as she was, and the few other people out on the street weren't of a sort likely to offer assistance. Where were the Literati officers when you actually needed them?

She quickened her pace, torn between trying to outrun the men and not getting too far away from the rendezvous. Given that she still wasn't that comfortable in heeled dress boots, she decided to continue as she was and hope they would lose interest.

What if Crimson had come and gone?

The thought made her stomach do flips.

The two men fell into step on either side of her. They smelled of liquor, vomit, and urine, a stench that didn't do much for her confidence. The one on the left had a crooked nose and a flat cap pulled low on his brow, shadowing his eyes. He wore no coat and had a knife at his belt. The man on her right wore a threadbare, tattered frock coat that he'd probably pulled out of some toff's ashbin.

"It ain't polite to ignore a bloke that's talkin' to ye."

"Nor is it proper to speak with strange men on the street," she returned sharply. The chill air had gone suddenly colder, as if a frost were on the way.

"It ain't real proper fer a young lass to be out on her own. Ye must be lookin' fer somethin' you oughtn't be."

"I can assure you that I'm not looking for you." *Crimson, now would be a fine time to show up. Please.*

The bloke in the frock coat grabbed her arm and she spun, jerking away, only to run into the man with the flat cap who had stepped around behind her. He took hold of her shoulders, his grip not painful, but far from gentle.

"How can ye know if ye don't give a bloke a try?"

The man in the coat stepped closer. Her heart felt like it was in her throat now. She reached back, felt the hilt of the knife on the other man's belt. She brought her knee up into the groin of the man in front, then brought her heel down hard on the foot of the man behind her. The man in front staggered backward and curled over, his hands cupped over his groin, his face flushing brightly.

The grip on her arms loosened and she spun away, taking the knife with her and holding it up in threat.

The man in the flat cap looked from her to his companion and back again, his eyes wide and a bit crazy. "Ye bloody harlot!"

"Leave me alone," she warned.

He sneered and lifted his leg to pull another, bigger knife from his boot.

Of course he would have another knife.

She shifted her stance, silently cursing the heavy folds of fabric that hung around her legs. The man in the coat had backed up into a wall and remained there, groaning. She'd landed a solid hit. The man in the flat cap shifted into a fighting stance that he looked all too comfortable with.

She heard the sound of hooves clattering on the cobbles moments before a coach drawing up behind him caught her eye, the two black horses wonderfully familiar.

In her second of distraction, the bloke darted in at her. She danced back and her heel caught the hem of the dress, almost taking her down. She grabbed out with her free hand and caught his arm, tipping him off balance as well. His blade cut a stinging shallow gash in her bicep.

She twisted, using the offset of his weight to regain her own balance, then let go. He stumbled past, catching his feet after a few staggering strides. She poised to fend him off when he turned, but this time he held up his hands and started to back away. Seconds later, Maeko saw why. Crimson walked up with a pistol in her hand and a finger on the trigger. Her emerald eyes flashed with hatred.

"You two boys best be on your way," Crimson warned.

The man with the flat cap backed up several steps, then turned and ran, leaving his companion behind. Crimson glanced at the second man who still didn't appear to be able to offer much threat and holstered her gun.

"Sorry I was late. Looks like you had things mostly under control though."

Maeko lowered the knife and pulled at the bloody slash in her dress sleeve. "Bugger ruined my dress."

Crimson laughed. "Come along. We'll have Marta see to the dress and your mother see to the cut."

On the ride back, Maeko pressed a handkerchief to the cut to stop the bleeding while she filled Crimson in on what she had gotten from Wells.

The woman shook her head and cursed under her breath. "This isn't good news, but we'll talk to Drake tomorrow and come up with a plan."

"Why not tonight?"

Crimson laughed lightly, shaking her head so that her mane of wavy red hair swayed back and forth. "You are a fierce little thing. It's late. If Drake isn't still out, he'll be asleep. Tomorrow will be here sooner than you realize."

Maeko accepted the answer with grudging reluctance. She rode along in silence, her arm stinging from the cut. Her fingers felt cool and tingly in the wake of the fight. Her heartbeat slowed toward normal.

Once they got back, they woke Tomoe to tend the shallow cut. She did so with her lips pursed tightly in disapproval the whole time, though she kept her thoughts to herself. Then, despite her eagerness to make progress, Maeko crawled into the bed and petted Macak while he lectured her for leaving without him. Then she drifted off to the sound of his purring.

#

It seemed like only minutes had passed when someone shook her gently awake.

"Mae."

Ash. "Are you in my room again?" She buried her face in the pillow.

"Looks that way."

"Is the sun out?" Her voice came out muffled by the pillow.

"No."

"Wake me when it is."

He exhaled a small chuckle. "You know this is London, right?"

She pulled the covers over her head.

"You know its noon, right?"

Noon! Why was she so sodding tired? She pulled

the covers off her head and rolled onto her side to look at him. "Is it really?"

He nodded.

"I need to talk to Drake." She pulled her arm out of the covers.

Ash caught her wrist, his eyes going to the fresh bandage. "What's that?"

"A little cut. It's nothing."

"What did you do last night when you went to town with Crimson?"

She pulled her arm away and rubbed her eyes. "Information gathering."

He sat on the edge of the bed, making the sheets pull tight across her. "Why won't you tell me what you're up to?"

"Because you don't like me taking risks."

"I'm not that daft. I know you're doing it, even if you don't tell me about it. Maybe I could be of some help."

She stared at the ornate ceiling and blew out a heavy breath. "I know. I have a feeling I could use your help on this next adventure anyway, but I have to talk to Drake first."

Without waiting for the request this time, Ash got up and retrieved her clothes for her. Then he moved away and stood with his back to her. Sometime while she was gone, Tomoe, apparently weary of seeing her scars, had hung blankets over all the mirrors in the room, so Maeko climbed out of the covers this time.

"Where's Macak?" She pulled her nightdress off.

"Your mum brought him out this morning. Crimson said some bloke wanted to look at the leg and took him off to do secret things only special people get to know about."

"Ash."

"Mae." He matched her exasperated tone perfectly.

She balled up the nightdress and threw it at him. It hit him in the head and landed by his feet. He glanced down at it.

"Do that again and I'll turn around and throw it back at you."

She began to pull her shirt on with renewed haste. "You wouldn't dare."

"Don't tempt me."

She hurried into the rest of her clothes. "Done. Do you know where Drake is?"

Ash turned. He gave her an appraising look. "Your hair is growing out fast. I like it longer."

She walked to the vanity and pulled a brush out of the drawer. Her hair was getting longer, which meant it was probably a mess. Ash walked up behind her and reached around to pull the blanket off the mirror, leaning in close enough that she could feel the warmth of him. Doing her best to ignore him, she started to rake the brush through her hair. He caught her hand and took the brush away.

She met his eyes in the reflection. "Don't."

"Shut up, sit down, and let me brush your hair." He pulled out the chair in front of the vanity. His look promised a war if she refused.

Reluctantly she sat, and he began to run the brush through her hair with far more care than she had. It felt lovely, but she had a purpose and she couldn't let anything distract her from it.

"Drake?"

"He's been in the second-floor study since he got back."

"Back?"

"Yes. He left with five other blokes not long after you left yesterday. He got back a few hours ago and vanished into the study with two of them. He looked really brassed off. Crimson joined them just before I came in here."

She glanced up sharply, meeting his pale eyes in the reflection again. "She didn't stay with Macak?"

He grinned. "Relax. They don't seem like the type of people who would torture cats."

"Neither did Lucian."

He stopped brushing and gave her a startled look. "What?"

"Nothing. It doesn't matter now." She took advantage of his pause and stood up. "I need to talk to Drake."

"I wouldn't go in there," he warned.

"You're not going to." She turned and hurried out the door, not giving him time to argue.

She heard the brush clatter down on the vanity as he hurried after her, falling into pace beside her in the hallway. "What do you need to talk to him about?"

"I'll tell you after I talk to him."

Anger started to flush his cheeks.

"Promise," Maeko said.

"Fine. I'll be waiting."

She nodded and made her way to the study. Ash stopped at the end of the hall and let her continue alone though she could feel his irritated gaze following her.

Outside the door, she hesitated for a moment. Should she knock? Probably so if she meant to stay in Drake's good graces. She knocked lightly.

Crimson opened the door. Maeko ducked in under her arm. She wasn't going to give them a chance to send her away. At least she had knocked.

Drake stood by one tall window staring out and two other haggard looking men stood near the desk in the center of the room. No one was sitting. An air of tension and frustration filled the room. Crimson pursed her lips and gave a tiny shake of her head at Maeko, but shut the door behind her.

Drake glanced over his shoulder at her then faced out the window again. He pressed his thumb against the bridge of his nose and closed his eyes, drawing in a deep breath. He looked tired. No, more than that, he looked disheartened.

"Maeko. Crimson already told me what you learned." He opened his eyes and continued to stare out the window. The other two men regarded her with sympathetic looks, and she felt a sinking in her chest. "I'm familiar with the facility in question. I had Captain Eli pass over it in an airship just yesterday. I'm afraid any rescue attempt would be much too risky."

That explained the sympathetic looks. Crimson placed a hand on her shoulder. She shook it off and moved around the side of the desk.

"Chaff and Garrett are both there. We have to help them. You promised."

Drake turned on her suddenly, the motion so quick and full of anger that she took a hurried step back.

"I lost two of my best men last night getting my

shipment back from the Literati. I will not needlessly risk more, not even for Garrett."

"And certainly not for some street rat," she hissed.

He gave her a hard look. "I'm sorry. It can't be done."

"I'll find a way."

"What will you do, grow wings and fly over the wall? You'll never get in and out of there without my help."

"I don't need your bloody help." She spun on her heel and stormed out, slamming the door as hard as she could behind her.

At the end of the hall, Ash jerked to attention, startling when the door slammed. Maeko met his eyes for a second, then turned and strode the other direction. It wasn't that she didn't want to talk to him, she just didn't want to risk lashing out at him in frustration. The sound of his rushed footsteps gained on her even as she walked briskly around to a door that led out onto a balcony overlooking the front courtyard and grounds.

She stormed through the door, leaving it open behind her since she knew shutting it wouldn't stop him, and walked to the railing. Cool air washed over her, quenching some of the fire of fury burning within.

He promised to help.

Her hands curled around the cold railing and she glowered out. Someone was working with a young horse in one of the paddocks, attempting to introduce it to a saddle. The animal danced away from the large leather object, tossing its head in a way that made it look as if it were mocking the man trying to saddle it.

You tell him. She smiled faintly, the fist of anger relaxing a little more.

Ash shut the door behind him and came to stand next to her. He gave her a cautious glance before speaking. "Care to tell me what happened in there?"

The man popped the horse's lead sharply and the animal tossed his head back, splaying his front feet wide in surprise. The man shook his head, set the saddle on the railing, and picked up a long whip. He then led the horse out into the middle of the paddock and drove the animal out to move around him in a big circle. She didn't know much about working with horses, but it appeared to calm the animal. After a few spirited kicks, the horse settled and fell into a steady stride.

"I found out last night where Chaff and Garrett are being held, but now Drake is refusing to help get them out."

Ash scowled. "See, he is an arse. We can't leave my dad…" He caught himself. "We can't leave them there."

The horse's movement was mesmerizing, his strides long and smooth, his mane and tail streaming behind him. The smelly beasts could be rather majestic at times.

She drew in a deep breath, letting it calm her. "No. He's right to refuse. He lost two men last night getting back some supplies the Lits got their hands on. It wouldn't be reasonable to expect him to risk more lives for this."

Ash gave her a worried look. "I don't like it when you start talking sense. Makes me wonder what plots are hatching in that brain of yours. I know you don't give up this easy."

Never have. She started to chew at the inside of her lip.

If Ash took his family and her mother away from here… Could she even get to Thaddeus without Bennett or Joel catching her first? It was a risk, one in which the consequences were dire. Bennett scared her. He had looked much too eager when Thaddeus suggested letting him have his way with her.

He was a killer, not because he needed to be one, she suspected, but because he liked being one. She might be able to convince Bennett to take her to Thaddeus if he found her, but that assumed a lot about his concern for his employer's wishes. She suspected his loyalty fell below his personal pleasures on a scale of importance. Besides, she'd only asked Thaddeus to free one person. He might not barter for more than that, which meant she needed to find another way if she meant to get Garrett out too.

Her gaze moved over the grounds and something caught her eye. The black nose of Drake's small airship stuck out from behind the nearest stable.

"Why is Drake's airship out?"

Ash looked at the end of the ship. "They moved it up this morning. One of the men said they needed the space below for something else."

They must have needed more space for assembling the battleship. That would be a sight to see, if Drake didn't ban her from the lower level after her show of temper. However, as long as Macak was down there, they would have to kill her to keep her out.

Ash was still gazing at the end of the ship, an almost feverish gleam in his eyes. "I'd love to fly that thing."

The gears began to spin faster in her head. "Would you?"

He turned to her. "Who wouldn't? You've flown it. Was it brilliant?"

She had to smile at his enthusiasm. "It was rather

splendid. Maybe you'll get a chance sometime."

Soon.

There was a light knock on the door behind them, a momentary warning before Crimson stepped out. She acknowledged Ash with a nod and focused on Maeko.

"I'm sorry, Kitten. I know Drake promised you…" She trailed off when Maeko held up a hand.

"He did, but he's right."

Crimson threw an alarmed glance in Ash's direction.

He returned a worried look. "Rather unsettling, isn't it."

Maeko ignored the exchange. "I still need to meet with my contact tomorrow night. I can't simply leave him hanging. He might have some other useful information. Do you think someone could alter my dress so it doesn't look like I only own one?"

Crimson sized her up with a glance and smirked. "I can do you one better. Drake's sister died of consumption when she was seventeen. Most of her clothes are still in her room. I don't think it would take much to make a few of the dresses fit you."

"Wouldn't that upset him? I think he's already peeved with me."

Crimson shook her head. "If you knew him better, you'd know he's more upset with himself. I've never seen him go back on his word before. He doesn't take losing someone lightly. Would it surprise you to learn that he suggested giving you some of her dresses the day after you got here? He hasn't said anything because he didn't think you would be any more willing to wear them than I would."

"Oh. They do come in handy on occasion. Don't

you ever wear dresses?"

Crimson wrinkled her nose. "No. He did buy me the loveliest gown once. I take it out now and then just to look at it."

"You should wear it for him sometime."

Crimson glanced at Ash again.

He shrugged. "I think maybe she's sick."

Maeko felt her face starting to flush. "Oh, bother. You two are impossible. Where are these silly dresses?"

They followed Crimson to an unoccupied room and began digging through dresses in the wardrobe of Drake's dead sister. Even living in the bedroom of Lucian's deceased daughter for a time hadn't accustomed her to the strange, pervasive sense of something missing that filled the room of someone who had passed away. It made her eager to depart. Crimson moved with the haste of someone who felt much the same. She pulled out the dresses and threw them down on the bed, quickly grabbing those that were clearly too formal for the task at hand and hanging them back up to narrow the options.

"This one's nice."

Ash held up a yellow dress with a big cascading bustle. Lace lined the bust as well as every seam and layer of fabric. Crimson wrinkled her nose and Maeko made a small sound of disgust.

"Perhaps you should wear it. I'm sure it would be lovely on," she teased.

He tossed the dress down and balled up a coffee colored jacket to throw at her. She caught it and held it up. There was a sedate black lace trim and the jacket itself had simple, fitted lines appropriate for eveningwear. Not too formal or fancy.

She lowered it to look over the top at Crimson. "What does this go with?"

Crimson dug through the pile and pulled out a dress of the same color, also sparingly trimmed in black lace.

They smiled at one another and spoke in sync. "Perfect."

A few hours later, after a thorough fitting to have the dress altered, Maeko and Ash sat in plush chairs in a quiet little tearoom hidden in one corner of the upper level. The walls were a pale yellow with a floral pattern that made Maeko cringe. Elaborately carved woodwork trim rippled around the windows and doors like waves of white foam. It almost looked edible.

What was edible was the selection of cakes and pastries they'd snagged from the kitchen and laid out on a small table between them. Custard tarts, pumpkin pasties—Maeko tried to make herself munch on them.

Large windows overlooked the pasture. A light rain fell outside, the sky slowly darkening with the onset of evening. Three horses stood under a tree in the pasture, their bay coats turning black as daylight sank away on the horizon. They stood quiet, each with one rear foot at rest, the occasional shift to the other foot or twitch of an ear the only movement to draw them out as something alive amidst the deepening shadows.

"They look sad." She looked at Ash as she spoke only to find him watching her.

He turned to glance down at the solemn beasts. "I don't think they're sad. They're just resting the way horses do."

"Oh." She gazed down on them again. "They

always look sad when it's raining."

"I imagine they like it better when it isn't." He popped a bite of pastry into his mouth and chewed.

Maeko held her silence. He wanted to talk about something. She could feel the unspoken words hanging heavy in the air, so she curled her legs up into the chair and waited. He swallowed the bite and started to reach for another, then stopped and returned his hand to the arm of the chair instead.

"You mean to go after them anyway, don't you?"

No point lying since she planned to give him his wish and let him help this time. "Yes."

"How?"

"It depends on what I learn tomorrow night. How would you feel about borrowing Drake's airship?"

He glanced at her out of the corner of his eye. "Without asking?"

"Of course."

"They call that stealing."

"I mean to return it." She popped a small lemon cake in her mouth.

He gazed out the window in thoughtful silence, but the slow change in the set of his jaw gave her all the answer she needed. He would help.

"Can I come with you tomorrow night?"

"I don't care if you ride in the coach, but I have to meet my contact alone."

"Why?"

"He's a Literati officer and I'm meeting him at JAHF. I can't exactly take my mates along." Not to mention Ash's presence would discourage Wells's coworkers convenient assumption that there was a relationship between them. The way things were, the late hour of her visits and her lack of chaperone would encourage the supposition that their courtship was being carried on in secret. Nothing distracted people away from the truth like a little sumptuous scandal.

Ash ran a hand through his dark hair, leaving it charmingly mussed. "Why can't you ever find a safe way to get things done?"

"I do the best I can. Besides, what fun would safe be?" She grinned and tossed a cake at him.

He caught it and gave her a sly grin, bounding up from his seat with the cake brandished before him like a weapon.

"Don't!"

She threw her hands up and he caught one wrist, parrying the other with the arm holding the cake as he drove the morsel toward her face. She twisted her arm, knocking the cake away at the last second and throwing his balance off. He tripped and went over, taking her and the chair with him. His leg caught the edge of the table, kicking it over, and the remaining selection of delicious pastries rained down on them. When Crimson opened the door to call them to dinner, she found them splayed on the floor coated with the remains of smashed sweets and laughing too hard to do anything about it.

Macak trotted into the room with Crimson, the gears in his leg clicking softly, and dutifully began to lick a bit of buttery pastry from Maeko's chin.

Maeko considered her reflection in the long mirror she had uncovered. The newly altered dress fit perfectly. The understated deep coffee color and simple style had a quiet elegance to it that she hadn't expected. It looked fully appropriate for a young lady out in the evening hoping to impress a possible suitor. To her surprise, with the assistance of a little corsetry and proper tailoring, she actually looked the part. That her black hair had grown out a bit didn't hurt the overall effect either.

Crimson helped her finish off the ensemble by pinning her hair up into a small bun and topping it off with a matching decorative little hat tilted neatly to one side. It proved that the woman's lack of feminine embellishments had nothing to do with a lack of ability.

When they finished, Crimson clapped her hands sharply. "Chivvy along now! We've got places to go!"

"And we don't want to give Drake a chance to spot us heading out."

"Precisely."

Maeko took a quick moment to cover the mirror for her mother's sake before turning to follow Crimson from the room. When she walked past the vanity, Macak leapt up to her shoulders. His claws dug in through the material. Extracting them would have to be carefully done to avoid damaging the dress, but she liked him there. His presence always boosted her confidence somehow.

Crimson turned before the door and held up a staying hand. "The cat stays here."

"He's bored."

"He's a cat."

"And I'm a rat." With a smirk, Maeko stepped around the other woman and opened the door, proceeding Crimson out with Macak happily balanced upon her shoulders.

Ash was already out front by the coach, standing to one side of the open door. He stared a little too long as she approached, his gaze openly approving. She flushed and climbed into the coach fast enough that Macak had to dig in deep to hold on, and she clenched her teeth against the pain.

"Stop gawking," Crimson chastised Ash as she followed Maeko in. "You look like you've never seen a young lady before."

Ash followed them in and smiled at Maeko who averted her gaze, refusing to acknowledge his appraisal or how it made her feel a bit giddy.

"Not one that lovely."

He sat next to her and she turned her full attention to petting Macak who had extracted his claws and climbed down into her lap.

Crimson gave the cat a sour look. "You'll have fur all over you by the time we get there. Give him to me."

Maeko reluctantly relinquished the cat. He yowled an initial protest, then settled as Crimson began to scratch his chin and Maeko dutifully brushed the cat hair off the dress. She did have a part to play tonight. After that was done, Macak could get all the hair he liked on the dress.

Ash reached across to scratch Macak's head then sat back in the seat. "How did you become a Pirate, Crimson?"

Crimson smiled and a certain wistfulness in the expression captured Maeko's curiosity.

"I don't know that I ever became a Pirate. My father was a blacksmith. Keeping the horses here shod was a full-time occupation. We lived on the property, and Drake and I spent a lot of time together. He had an interest in science and engineering that I shared, so he brought me into the workshop his parents had set up for him and taught me everything he learned. At some point, the friendship turned into love. Whatever he is, I support him. If that makes me a Pirate, so be it."

Maeko straightened a bit of black lace on one sleeve of the jacket, making a point of not looking in Ash's direction as she spoke. "How did you fall in love with him?"

"I don't know. I just know that one day I realized that I wanted to be more than a friend to him. Fortunately, he felt the same. He's very private though. The Drake I fell in love with stays well hidden. In front of others he can be…" she hesitated, looking down at Macak's false leg as if the word she sought might be etched in its gleaming surface.

"Creepy," Maeko offered.

Crimson laughed. "Sometimes. He tries to take care of those who follow him, but he also tries not to get too close. He's lost many good mates."

Good mates who trusted him and followed him the way Chaff had followed her into danger and paid the price. Drake might not be willing to risk his own people to help her save Chaff, but he couldn't claim not to understand why she had to try.

Ash and Crimson were both against letting her do much walking alone in the city dressed as she was, especially after Crimson mentioned the blokes who had accosted her on the prior visit. After some argument, they agreed on a pickup location and dropped her off a block away from JAHF. If all went according to plan, it would be a short visit. She strode down the street and up the steps doing her best to move with the proper blend of the haste of secrecy and the confidence of privilege.

The older gentleman with the gap-toothed smile answered the door and, after glancing up and down the street, welcomed her in with a small, disapproving shake of his head.

"Pardon my asking, miss, but shouldn't you have a chaperone?"

She gave a shy smile. "My chaperone has fallen ill. I talked father into letting me go out. It is JAHF, after all. What could happen here?"

The gentlemen raised his brows, his expression suggesting that she might be surprised, but he said nothing as he shuffled back to his chair and sat down. He looked up at again once he had settled at his post. "Officer Wells is busy. If you wish to wait, I believe his visitor will be leaving shortly."

"Visitor?"

"Don't fret, Miss. You're the only lady what comes

to visit him here. He's meeting with Mr. Folesworth."

Her heart leapt into her throat. Fret? She wasn't going to fret, but she might panic. The telltale coach hadn't been out front. If it had been, she would never have come inside. Maybe his driver had parked around the side.

She deliberately unclenched her hands and smoothed her skirt. She couldn't be here when Thaddeus came out, but maybe she didn't have to leave either. "Is there somewhere quiet I could wait for him? Perhaps somewhere a bit warmer than here by the doors." She rubbed her arms with her hands for emphasis, her palms whispering over the fine material.

The man exhaled a monumental sigh and rose from his desk, a slow and laborious task, like watching an old arthritic cow trying to stand up after a long rest in the field. He shuffled to the inner doors and gestured for her to follow. She went after him, struggling not to fidget impatiently at his slow pace.

Shuffle faster.

Wouldn't it be lovely to run into Thaddeus at JAHF? He could simply lock her in a cell and be done with it. Although, she had the feeling he wanted her out of the way in a more permanent fashion. Merely locking her up and walking away wouldn't be enough.

The man let her into an office much like the one she'd last spoken to Wells in. He gestured toward a chair.

She offered him a tiny curtsy. "Thank you, Sir."

"Don't touch anything," he replied gruffly.

A door opened and shut somewhere nearby. She wanted to yell at him to shut the door, but she managed a polite smile.

"Of course not."

He nodded once more and left her, relief collapsing over her as the door clicked shut behind him. She sidled quickly over and put her ear to the crack.

"You're sure you wouldn't prefer the day shift. There are plenty of openings."

That was Thaddeus. If she ever wanted to catch him and offer him an exchange for Chaff's life, this was the best chance she was going to get. He wouldn't kill her in front of Wells... probably. He would have to hear her out. She placed a hand on the doorknob.

"No, Sir. I've gotten rather used to the night shifts. I'd rather keep to the schedule I'm on, I just want off the streets for a while."

"Certainly. With the current unrest, I completely understand. Leave the streets to the fresh blood. I need more men with a steady disposition keeping things in line at the new facility."

She pulled her hand away from the knob. Why was Thaddeus recruiting for the new facility? Was he that deeply enmeshed in Literati law enforcement?

"I'd be pleased to help, Sir."

"Welcome aboard then, Officer Wells. I'll make the transfer effective immediately. You can start tomorrow and your old partner, Tagmet, can help you get situated."

"Thank you, Sir."

The voices faded away as they passed through to the doors to the front. She sat, fidgeting restlessly with the lace that trimmed the jacket. How far could she trust Wells? He seemed a good upstanding sort, but that meant he'd be all the more likely to turn on her if he believed she was in the wrong and, given his profession and her history, it wouldn't take much to make him believe that.

The door opened and she hopped to her feet to hide her startle. Wells leaned on the door and looked her up and down once, his expression guarded.

"You realize the other officers think I'm courting you."

She shrugged. "I never said as much. I never discouraged the assumption either. It seemed like a good cover."

He walked into the room, stopping to close the door and flick the lock on the way in. "At least they think I have good taste, if a bit unconventional."

"I... They do?"

"You clean up nice enough," he replied, avoiding her eyes.

She surprised herself with a laugh. "So do you."

He shook his head, but his lips curved up with the hint of a smile.

Enough banter, they had business to conduct and she needed answers. "Why is Thaddeus in charge of recruiting for the new facility?"

He gave her a startled look.

She stared back at him for a second, replaying her own words in her head. *Oh.* "You still think that man is Lucian?"

"I'm afraid I never knew either brother well enough to tell the difference. Makes it awful hard to believe the wild things that have been said." He pulled a large folded paper out of the desk and set it down, placing one hand on top of it.

"Is someone at least investigating him?"

His silence was answer enough.

Rage bubbled up and to overflowing. She slammed a hand on the desk. "This is rubbish! How can you let him get away with this?"

With unshaken composure, he slid the paper across the desk. "This is a map of the new facility. After I talked to you, I asked if they had openings there. Told them I was tired of working the streets. I went out earlier today for a tour of the place. I start work there tomorrow night. If you can give me at least two nights to get the details worked out, I can get you into the right building, but you have to get past the wall on your own. I don't see how you expect to—"

"I can handle that," she interrupted, struggling to sound confident as she reached out for the map.

He slid it back to his side before her fingers made contact. "I'm not doing this for free."

C H A P T E R   E I G H T

She stared at the map, fighting the urge to grab it. Might she be able to talk Drake into giving her the money for whatever bribe he expected? Without telling him why she needed the money, she doubted it. It didn't matter though. She knew many ways to get her hands on some tin if it came to that. "How much?"

"I'm not asking for money. I'll have to abandon my post to get you into the right building and that isn't going to look so good. If I help you get in and out of there, you have to promise to take me with you and give me sanctuary."

She stared at him, aware that her mouth was hanging open. She shut it. "*You* want to join the Pirates?"

"Not in the least. I just want out of here. I don't like the way things are being done."

How brassed off would Drake be if she brought a Lit officer back with her? She swallowed back a grin. "It's a deal."

"That easy?"

She nodded. Once he was at the stronghold, what could Drake do? He had to take him in. She couldn't promise Wells he wouldn't end up locked in a room, but he would be away from the Lits. Anything had to be an improvement.

He unfolded the map. It covered much of the table. The facility it revealed, surrounded by a wall that would do many castles proud, was very big. Two huge buildings took up most of the center on either side of an open yard. Four smaller buildings, each big enough themselves to house two of the JAHF buildings, were set along the inside of one wall. Two long narrow buildings occupied the same space along the opposite wall. Guard towers stood at each corner as well as in the middle of the two longer stretches of wall.

Wells pointed to the second in the run of the four smaller buildings. "Chaff is here, in the medical building. They have Garrett housed in the next building over."

Her chest twisted with remorse and guilt. They must still be tending Chaff's injured hand if they had him in the medical building. "What are those big buildings?"

"Research and development. They're factories for Mr. Folesworth's weapons designs and several other projects he's working on. They didn't show me inside either of them."

That cleared up Folesworth's involvement a bit. "He's using the prisoners as free labor?"

Wells gave a sharp nod. He looked a shade paler than normal all of a sudden. "Labor and as test subjects for experiments."

"Experiments? What experiments?"

"We can talk more about that after you get me out of there. For now, if you can get to the door on this side of the medical building I can let you in." He pointed to the side nearest the wall then looked up at her expectantly.

She nodded, ignoring the dread that set her nerves jittering.

"Good. Be there ten minutes after midnight on this coming Friday night. I'll check twice after that if you aren't there on time. Any more than that and I'm likely to be noticed. We'll get your boy Chaff and I'll see what I can do to get Garrett out too." He flipped the map over. "I've written out directions from the city here. I don't know what side you're approaching from, but you should be able to find it with this information."

"Thank you."

Wells started to fold the map again. "Don't thank me. Like as not, we'll all be killed or worse."

Worse than killed? Maybe it was best not to ask. Her nerves were already on fire.

He finished folding the map and handed it to her. She folded it a few more times and tucked it up under her bodice as he escorted her out. At the front door, she turned and gave him a peck on the cheek again. The gesture might be highly inappropriate and might lead to teasing from the other officers, but it would keep their assumptions far away from the truth.

The coach should have been waiting down a side street a few dark, lonely blocks away, but tonight there was no one around to bother her. The city felt like it slept, waiting for something to wake it, like a warrior resting up before battle. The streets near JAHF were eerily quiet. Perhaps they were always that way, given the presence of the jail, but the feeling prompted her to a faster walk. She slowed coming around the last corner, though the two men standing near Drake's coach spotted her at the same moment she spotted them. Her initial alarm faded when she recognized Detective Emeraude's two assistants.

Was it bold, or merely stupid, for them all to be rendezvousing this close to JAHF?

Reuben tipped his hat and Amos smirked at her. She nodded to them each and Rueben opened the door for her when she got to the coach. Em sat alone on one seat, across from Crimson and Ash, making the only available space Maeko could take next to Em, at least without conspicuous crowding on the opposite seat.

Maeko gave a curt nod in response to Em's scowl and sat, taking a moment to smooth her dress in the hopes that the detective might declare her purpose and give Maeko some information to work with before she was forced to say anything.

Crimson broke the awkward silence. "I understand you two headstrong birds are already acquainted."

Em pursed her lips and said nothing.

Maeko matched her silence.

"That would be a resounding yes. Amazing how loud you two can be in your silence."

"I've got work to do," Em stated, moving around Maeko to toss the door open. "I'll be in touch."

"I'm sure you will. Shall I say hello to Drake for you?" Crimson added the last with a sugary tone.

Em turned back with such fury in her eyes that Maeko almost jumped up to defend Crimson. There was some kind of unpleasant history between them. That much had become immediately, painfully clear.

"Tell him to go hang himself." Em stepped out and swept the door firmly closed.

"Always a pleasure," Crimson intoned softly to the

closed door and knocked twice on the roof of the coach. The coach wheels creaked as it began to roll.

She eyed Maeko. "Since you two are clearly on better terms than she and I," Maeko almost choked at that, "perhaps I'll send just you to meet with her next time."

"Oh, of course. That makes perfect sense." She meant it to be sarcastic, but Crimson only nodded as if it had been decided. Maeko sighed inwardly. "What did she want?"

"She's been talking with the new metropolitan police commissioner. Seems they aren't happy with the cooperation they've been getting from the Literati in regards to the murder of the former commissioner. Em has been trying to convince the commissioner to launch an investigation into your claim that the wrong Mr. Folesworth died in that airship explosion. They haven't gone for it yet, but she says she thinks the ongoing difficulties with the Literati police force are pushing them toward considering it."

Macak, who had been crouched down alongside Ash while Em was there, moved over to curl on Maeko's lap. She began to pet him, and his deep purr melted away some of the tension Em had left behind. "The Bobbies don't even have jurisdiction in the city anymore, do they?"

"Not precisely, but there may be a loophole they can leverage given the nature of the case and the current unrest in the city. Em came to ask if we might be able to increase the pressure on the Lits. Cause a few more high profile incidents and the like. I told her it was Drake's call, since it would require putting more people at risk. That brassed her off a bit."

"She obviously doesn't like Drake much?"

Crimson shifted the curtain over the window to one side, gazing out into the dark night while she spoke. "Her brother was a Literati officer. He worked closely with Drake on the sly, feeding him inside information like your contact is doing for you now. There was a protest that got ugly. He got into the middle of it, trying to stop it before people he cared about on either side got hurt. That's the danger of split loyalties. He was shot and killed. She blames the Lits and the Pirates equally for his death, but she decided that Drake deserved a little more blame than anyone else because he and her brother were very close."

At least there was something behind all that bitterness. "I think she extends that blame to just about everyone she meets."

Crimson crossed her arms and sat back in the seat, a tight smirk twisting her lips. "You may be right. What did you find out from your Lit?"

Maeko also leaned back in the seat, letting the shadows of the coach obscure her features. If she told Crimson the plan, it might get back to Drake who would never allow them to go through with it, especially when he found out she meant to use his airship to get past the wall. The quiet, black ship would be the only thing that could get them inside the walls without too much risk of being seen. Even then, it was chancy, but what else could she do. She had to get to Chaff.

"He says it can't be done." She put a strong dose of pouty disappointment into her tone for authenticity.

"What?" Judging by the burst of anger in Ash's voice, the show was somewhat convincing. "That can't be right. We have to get in there."

He slapped his fist into his palm in a show of stubborn determination that she quietly admired.

Crimson put a hand on his arm. "Asher, we can't do the impossible. Your father and Maeko's friend are going to have to take care of themselves for now. Drake means for us to come out on the top of this conflict. When we do, we'll get them back."

Maeko chewed at her lip. How reasonable Crimson made it sound, as if there were no doubt at all that the Pirates would succeed and the two prisoners would be fine until then. Maeko barely understood what they were fighting for. They wanted to stop the Lits from gaining more power and increasing the class separation that was already crippling the city's poor. They wanted to give people more rights and help the growing numbers who were being forced into workhouses or driven to the streets. That seemed noble enough, but what was the solution? Clashes in the streets didn't really change anything, not that she could see. They mostly led to innocent people getting hurt. What did it mean for them to win?

"I'd venture that the Lits mean to come out on top too."

Crimson gave her a sharp look.

Maeko shrugged.

Ash switched seats and slumped back into the corner, glowering through the window. If things kept on the way they were, he would be as pleasant to be around as Em soon. Perhaps, when he learned the truth, he'd cheer up. She had to tell him. There was no way to manage the infiltration alone. If it were foggy, they'd be able to bring the ship in closer. A clear night meant they'd be lucky to get within drop range without detection. Either way, someone had to man the ship while she went in to meet Wells.

Drake was right to say no. He might not mourn her and Ash so much if something happened to them, but he would undoubtedly mourn his airship. Not only that, she suspected the ship was a legitimate purchase, which meant the Lits could trace it back to him. She hoped he'd have the sense to declare it stolen if something went wrong, and there was plenty that could go wrong.

She began to chew at a fingernail and Ash reached up, taking her hand and pushing it back down to her side. That he didn't attempt to keep hold of it said a lot for the unpleasantness of his mood. They would be back at the estate soon though. Then she could tell him the truth.

R ain poured down with all the ferocity of a waterfall in flood. It wasn't the fog she had been hoping for, but it would drown out the sound of the quiet airship in addition to reducing visibility, which made it better even if it was right dreadful to be out in. Maeko slunk out across the grounds, moving stealthily from building to building, then slipped behind the stable to where the black airship waited. She cracked the airship door, glancing around for any unexpected occupants, and darted inside, eager to get out of the downpour.

The curtains were drawn over all the airship windows to hide the dim light of a single candle flickering in the darkness of the interior. Ash stood near the controls, waiting for her. He must be at least as anxious to get going as she was given that he'd beat her there and, judging by his pale countenance and the grim expression, was at least as dubious about their chances for success.

He held the candle out toward her, then looked down to her right and his brow furrowed. "Why did you bring the cat?"

"I didn't." She glanced down.

Macak shook himself with a look of annoyance, sending a fine spray of water out in a circle around him. Then he trotted past her to hop up on one of the plush chairs and settled in to groom the water from his fur.

"Sneaky devil," she commented, feeling a burst of pride. She walked over to the control panel. "You know how to fly this thing?"

"It looks straightforward enough and you've flown it. I'm sure we can manage together." He glanced over his shoulder. "Shouldn't we put the cat back in the house?"

"The cat has a name," she grumbled. "And no. Sneaking out once was risky enough. We can't chance sneaking back in and out again for that. He'll just have to ride along."

Ash began to fiddle with the controls, preparing to let off air to take the ship up. Maeko trotted around the interior and freed the anchor attachments. Normally they would detach them from the outside and reel in the ropes, but since they wouldn't be anchoring again until they got back, she didn't see much point in going to the trouble to run around in the rain again. When the attachments were free, Ash began to take the ship up.

"It's like a child's toy—it's so easy!"

She grinned at the delight in his voice, then jumped a good foot when the door swung open and someone leapt up into the ship.

"Crimson!"

"You are nothing short of dangerous, Kitten," Crimson said. She jerked the door shut and turned to stare Maeko in the eyes.

The accusing look made her feel unconscionably guilty. She tugged Chaff's coat tighter around her shoulders, a move that earned her a frown from Ash, and stepped away from the svelte pillar of flame that had joined them in the gondola. She braced for a verbal beating.

Crimson smiled wryly.

"You remind me of Em when she was younger. Come on." She moved to the controls. "Better get this thing out of here fast if you want to avoid getting caught. Drake might shoot the ship down before he let some thief make off with it."

Maeko shared an incredulous look with Ash. "You don't mean to stop us?"

"No." Crimson gave her a perplexed look, as if the very notion were ludicrous. "You're going to find some way to try this. The best I figure I can do is try to keep you from getting yourselves killed in the process. Though why you brought the cat, I'll never guess."

"Macak," Maeko corrected.

"What?"

"Nothing." She gave Macak an apologetic look. At least she'd tried. He was too busy licking away the wet to notice.

Crimson and Ash turned their full attention to moving the ship up and away from Drake's property as fast as they could. Maeko sat in a chair to watch. The two hadn't spent that much time around each other and yet they turned the process into a remarkably harmonious dance. They worked the controls together with a cooperation that looked practiced. Perhaps their mutual fascination with machinery was what made it work so well. She began to unfold the map, then flipped it over on a small flat table next to some of the chairs. When the ship was clear of the estate, Crimson joined her there to look over the instructions Wells had given.

Based on the directions, she gave Ash guidance on their heading, then she had Maeko flip it to the map of the facility.

She whistled softly to herself. "This place looks like a fortress. You know you two are mad to try this, right?"

Maeko looked up at her. "Doesn't that make you just as mad?"

"I've never claimed otherwise." Her tone was flippant, though her tight-lipped stare and the one finger tapping on the control panel spoke to how seriously she took the situation. "We'll have no way to know if we've been spotted or not until we're already committed to the drop. Ash should be able to keep the ship out of visual range in this weather while we go down, but you and I won't have much hope of escape if they do spot us."

Maeko slapped a hand down on the middle of the map and pulled it close to her, drawing Crimson's attention with it. "Wait a minute. Since when are you coming down there with me?"

Ash glanced over his shoulder at them. "I think it's a good idea."

You would. Maeko scowled at him, but he had already turned his attention back to the ship. "There's no point putting both of us in danger. Wells is only expecting me."

"This ship is designed as a single pilot pleasure vessel. If something goes wrong, Ash can make it back to the estate without help. On the other hand, if something goes wrong on your end, it's likely to be something you can't handle alone. I'm armed and I'm a damn good shot. You want me with you."

Maeko sat back and shook her head. "I still don't think it's a good idea. Besides, Drake would kill both of us if something happened to you."

"Mae."

She glanced over at Ash. There was an unyielding look in his eyes when he turned around to face them.

"What?"

"If you expect me to be the pilot for this venture, I suggest you go along with Crimson."

She could only stare, her mouth slightly open, at a loss for words. Had he just given her an ultimatum? He had, and worse, it was one she couldn't argue with if she wanted this to work. Someone had to stay behind and fly the ship.

Crimson grinned and tipped an imaginary hat to him. "Thanks, Captain."

Ash gave a quick nod and turned back to the controls. Macak trotted over and hopped up on the control panel. He sat delicately to one side and watched Ash's hands with open curiosity, one paw rising slightly as if he considered batting at them.

Maeko looked down at the map. She pointed to a semicircle on the building Chaff was supposed to be in. "I'm supposed to meet Wells at the back door of this building. If we come down on the roof, we can climb down this exterior access ladder…"

Crimson started to shake her head. "No. I think we'd be better off to come down on the inner edge of the next building over. It's farther from the nearest watchtower. We'll have to keep the ship as high as we can, so we may have to leave a bit of a drop at the end, though it can't be enough that we make too much noise when we hit the roof. In this downpour, the sounds from this ship shouldn't alert anyone and it should be almost impossible to see, but the farther up we can keep it until it's time for pickup, the better."

"What about the pickup?"

"Same place. Unfortunately, in this weather, we won't be able signal our captain."

Maeko nodded. "We thought of that. All we came up with was to have him lower down at ten minute intervals and, if I wasn't back within an hour, he'd assume something went wrong and leave."

Crimson pressed her lips together and tapped a finger on the map. Ash's posture stiffened visibly. He didn't like that part of the plan, but there was no other logical way to deal with it, unless…

"What if you stayed on the roof? You could use tugs on the ladder to signal him. You'd have to stay out in this weather, but Ash wouldn't have to operate devoid of information that way and, if things go awry, at least one of us might have a chance to get out of there."

Crimson held Maeko's eyes. Ash was silent, but he didn't need to say anything. They'd argued over the possibility of him having to leave her behind and she didn't trust him to do so. Crimson, on the other hand, was far more likely to make a sensible decision and could ensure that Ash left if it were necessary. It would also mean only one person would be sneaking around the buildings, which halved the chances of being spotted.

"Can you shoot a gun?"

The hairs on Maeko's neck stood up. She had shot a

gun. When they rescued Lucian Folesworth from his traitorous partner, Joel, she had shot an officer to save Ash and had managed to shoot Joel in the leg. Both shots had hit the targets out of luck more than any skill at aiming and she hadn't liked doing it, even if it had helped save their lives. "I'd probably shoot myself in the foot. I'll just have to rely on Wells for protection if it comes up."

"And you're sure this Officer Wells isn't setting us up?"

Not entirely. "Yes."

"All right. Sounds like we've got a plan."

The words sparked off Maeko's nerves. For the remainder of the flight they worked out a series of ladder tugs Crimson could use to convey different information to Ash, including a way for them to signal before they started climbing up so he would have warning if someone else tried to come up. Only Macak looked calm, and even he sat observing from the side of the control panel with an uncommon stillness, his tail now wrapped around in front of his feet.

The facility, when they drew close enough to see the watchtower lights, looked almost twice as big as Drake's massive estate. Spotlights shone down from the towers and from the wall at intervals, mostly aimed to the ground outside the perimeter. The interior between the buildings was very dark, with only a few lamps placed at intervals to light walkways and over the main entrances. Not one of the lights aimed up. Apparently, they didn't expect the type of folks who could afford airships to be dropping in at the new prison unexpectedly. That made it possible for them to do a cautious high pass to get the lay of the area, though the heavy rain made it hard to make out details or tell for certain if anyone was patrolling outside the buildings.

As they came around, Ash shut off the main engines and began a gradual descent, drawing air slowly into the ballonets to lower them down. Maeko switched from chewing at her fingernails to chewing on the inside of her lip and back again while she peered down through one of the anchor latch doors to watch for activity below.

Crimson stood behind Ash, offering the occasional suggestion, but mostly watching in silence. She finally placed a hand on his shoulder. "That's probably far enough."

The ship steadied and Maeko turned the wheel to release the hatch. Crimson came to join her, crouching down to pull the rolled ladder out of its compartment in the floor. When the hatch was open, she tossed the bundle, letting it unroll by its own weight.

"I'm armed. I'll drop down first. Give me two minutes before you start down."

Maeko nodded, unable to speak for a moment. Her throat had tightened with fear now that the plan was in action. This was madness and felt more outrageous with every passing second, but she had to try. She watched, admiring the way Crimson started down the ladder without any hesitation. Then she took Chaff's jacket off and laid it gently over a chair. It was a little warmer than the light jacket she wore underneath, but the too-long sleeves might get in her way and she couldn't afford to be clumsy. Very soon, she would be able to give it back to him.

She walked over to where Ash still manned the controls. He was fiddling, making small adjustments. The controls didn't really need all the attention he was giving them while the ship was hovering there, but it probably calmed his nerves to be doing something.

He spun to face her, his gaze unusually solemn. "Promise me you'll make it back."

"Ash, I can't…"

His fingers came up to touch her cheek.

"Please. Just promise." His pale green eyes shone feverishly bright and moist with worry.

If that was what he needed to hear she could say the words. It wasn't as if she needed to worry about a confrontation should she break the promise. She swallowed her arguments.

"I promise."

He exhaled shakily and leaned close with obvious intent. She let him kiss her this time, a light kiss that stirred a painful longing in her chest. For a moment, with their lips touching, she yearned to give in to the driving need to feel safe and wanted, but he moved away before she could act on the impulse.

He lowered his gaze, avoiding her eyes, and turned back to the controls. "Be careful."

"You too, Captain."

That got a faint smirk. She scratched Macak's chin then walked to the hatch and turned around to step down onto the ladder. The cat followed her to the hatch, but, for once, he didn't try to come along. The pouring rain and the drop were apparently enough to discourage him, or perhaps he thought Ash might need his calming companionship.

The rungs were slippery in the rain. It was like climbing into an abyss with the dark pressing in on all sides, at least until she looked around and spotted the faint light of a watchtower. She preferred the feel of a black abyss. The tower light reminded her once again how much they were risking acting out a sketchy rescue plan, a plan of her devising, which meant the consequences were hers to bear.

At the bottom of the long climb, she had to hang from the last rung and even then it was a few foot drop to the roof.

Crimson was there to steady her when she landed. "I took a quick look over the sides. I don't see any guards out. Could be they don't run many patrols or it could be that the patrols are hiding from this blasted weather. Regardless, be careful climbing down. You'll be completely exposed while you're on the ladder."

Maeko only nodded, afraid Crimson might veto the whole effort even now if she heard the fear in her voice. The airship ladder began to rise, quickly vanishing from sight in the downpour. Crimson walked with her to the ladder on the side of the building. They both crouched at the edge and watched for a moment. Listening was almost useless with the heavy rain pounding on the rooftop. Sight was only marginally better given the limited lighting within the grounds, but at least they were inside the wall now.

I'm coming, Chaff.

R eady?"

Maeko nodded again.

"I'll watch your progress from here. Until you get inside, I can still help you. After that, you'll have to rely on your Lit friend."

Maeko hesitated.

Friend?

She doubted Wells would call her a friend and, if she were honest, she didn't consider him one either. Desperation drove her to trust him, and the fact that he'd helped her once in the past, letting her go when it had been his job to arrest her. He might not be a friend, but he wasn't an enemy either. That had to be good enough.

She delayed a moment, scanning for signs of movement in the rain while she gathered her nerves. When she still spotted nothing, she forced herself to turn and back over the side. The metal rungs on this ladder were more slippery than the rungs on the airships ladder. Only a few steps down, her feet slipped off and she smacked her chin on a rung, slamming her teeth together. Clinging with her arms, she brought her feet up and stood there for several seconds, trembling with more than the cold. Pain sharpened her awareness and she tested her footing with care before she continued.

Halfway down, she stopped again, and secured her grip before glancing down to check for guards. She froze when she spotted a figure striding around the corner of the building, about to pass directly under her. Rain tickled down the back of her neck, rolling under the collar of her light fitted jacket. She held her breath and kept still, a skill she'd perfected over her many years living on the streets and hiding from Lits. The man didn't slow, undoubtedly eager to get back in out of the rain.

After he passed around the other corner, she dared to breathe. She counted to sixty once before resuming her precarious descent. When her feet touched down on the sopping ground she almost laughed with relief, but silence was her friend here. Keeping quiet, she hurried around the side of the building, staying to the darkest shadows until she finally had to dart across to the neighboring building. Then she made her way around the backside between the wall and the building.

Here the lights from the nearest watchtower illuminated part of the walkway, but the contrast made the shadowed side even darker, so she stayed to that side until she reached the door. She scanned the area one last time then stepped into the light to press an ear to the crack around the door. The heavy rain made it unlikely that she'd hear anything, but it was worth a listen just in case. With one hand, she gently pressed down on the lever. It shifted a fraction before she met resistance. Locked.

What was she supposed to do, knock?

The handle moved suddenly and she sprang back into the shadows. The door opened and Wells leaned out. His face was deathly pale. His eyes squinted ahead, trying to adjust enough to see into the shadows. Her gut trembled as she forced herself to step into the light.

He drew in a sharp breath. "Miss Maeko. You made it past the wall. I almost hoped you wouldn't come."

"So did I."

He held the door open and she hurried past him into the building. The stark empty hallway was dark, but light shone in from one side towards the end. She turned to find Wells staring down the hall alongside her. His nervous energy was almost palpable and it made her skin crawl.

"There's been a little complication."

The words caused a sinking in her gut. "What?"

"Chaff is in this building, though moving him isn't going to be easy as I hoped, but Garrett has been moved across the grounds to a building I don't have access to. They took him over there earlier this evening to work on some special project. They're also moving his quarters to one of the other buildings."

"Why?"

"They decided to grant him more comfortable quarters since he's been cooperating."

Alarm made her heart jump. She gave him a startled look.

"Don't worry. He hasn't given them any information as far as I can tell. They put him to work on some inventions and Mr. Folesworth is pleased with the results so far. Unfortunately, right now he is in the building with the research and development facilities. It's the most heavily guarded building on the grounds. I'm sorry. There's no way I can get in there."

"You're sure?"

Wells nodded. "At least he's safe. They aren't going to hurt him. He's the best engineer they've got."

There was no way around it then. Garrett would have to stay here for now. Ash was going to be devastated, but he would have to understand.

She was reminded of when she and Chaff failed to save Ash's little brother from the orphanage. He hadn't been so understanding about that. She hoped they had both learned enough since then that this wouldn't be quite so difficult, but that hadn't been so long ago, even if it did feel like an age had passed since.

"Where's Chaff?"

Wells started walking and she followed him, keeping her steps light and quiet on the bare floors.

He glanced back. "Don't worry. There are only two other officers stationed in this building tonight and they're both sleeping off the special batch of coffee I made them."

She couldn't hold back a grin. Wells wasn't so bad at this. "Brilliant thinking."

She relaxed a little, though it was hard not to pause and listen in each doorway as they worked their way deeper into the building. The stark hallways all looked the same, with rows of doors on either side. Many were simply numbered, some kind of short term holding cells perhaps. Others bore plaques declaring their purpose. They passed a disturbing number of surgery and exam rooms given that it was supposed to be merely a prison, as well as a few storage rooms and the like before Wells came to a sudden stop and turned to face the door of room number 27. He picked up a small satchel that sat on the floor alongside the door.

"What's that?"

He drew a set of keys out of one pocket, staring at them with evasive intensity while he answered. "A few things you might need to care for him. Some morphine, some clean bandages, and a few other medical supplies."

Unease pricked at the back of her mind and her mouth went dry. Something wasn't right. Wells had been holding something back. "For his hand?"

"Yes." He shifted his feet and avoided her attempt to catch his eyes.

A sick feeling began to swell in her gut. "How bad is it?"

"I thought it might be easier to show you." He slid back a panel in the door, revealing an observation window.

She peered in and caught her breath. Horror tightened her chest.

Chaff lay on a camp bed, his wrists and ankles bound down with wide straps, his eyes closed and his bare chest barely moving. He looked gaunt and sweat beaded on his flushed skin. The hand that had been shot was wrapped, but the skin on his wrist and arm above the wrap was swollen and turning a dark red, almost black right above the wrap.

"What did they do to him?"

Wells winced. "When he refused to give them information about the Pirates—"

"He didn't know anything about the bloody Pirates. He was only there because of me."

Wells put a hand on her shoulder. "Easy. Keep your voice down. We don't want to draw attention."

She shoved his hand away. "You said they're asleep."

"No point taking chances." He looked around once, held his breath to listen, then exhaled softly, turning a pitying expression on the still figure beyond the window. "He said he didn't know anything, but they didn't believe him. When he refused to give them any information, they told him they would stop treating his hand until he either changes his mind or the infection kills him."

"He was just trying to help me." A surge of bile in the back of her throat forced her to swallow hard. How he would resent pity from a Lit. "Why is he so still?"

"He was shouting and moaning a lot, so they started giving him heavy doses of morphine and the occasional application of chloroform to keep him quiet."

Rage welled, the edges of her vision turning red. She gave Well's a furious look. "Are they trying to kill him?"

The officer's jaw tightened convulsively and a hint of anger narrowed his eyes. "If he doesn't give them any information, I believe they do intend to let him die this way. I found an undated entry in the back of his file that reads 'died of unpreventable complications.'"

How could anyone watch someone die this way? She drew in a deep breath to combat the agony that twisted in her chest. Her throat hurt. *I did this to him.*

"Why is he strapped down?"

"The file says he has been very hostile throughout his stay here."

That was probably an understatement if she knew Chaff. She gave a wry and distinctly unladylike snort.

"Hostile. What did they expect? They're leaving him to die from infection." She nodded to the keys dangling from Wells' fingers. "Let's get him out of here."

"The smell from the infection is rather unpleasant." He warned, then added, "be careful when we undo the restraints. He's feverish, and they've got him drugged up. He might not recognize you right off."

"He'll recognize me."

Her hands had started to shake. She balled them into fists by her sides to try to keep them still while Wells unlocked the door. When the door was open, they were greeted by the gagging stench of infection. They rushed in against that overwhelming stink. Chaff didn't stir, though his breathing changed ever-so-slightly for a few seconds. Wells went to his ankles to start unbuckling the straps. Maeko hastily went to work on the strap on his injured arm, feeling intense heat in his skin as she unbuckled it, then she darted around to free the other one.

Bastards!

The moment the healthy arm was free, his hand shot up and closed around her throat. Chaff sat up part way, his glassy, unfocused eyes staring into her face, lips twisting in a grimace. The hand tightened, trying to crush her windpipe. She clawed at the fingers, remembering the crude fake arm of the thug who'd attacked her in the alley and how impervious it had been to her struggles. Chaff had saved her then. Now, drugged and feverish, it was his hand choking her, impervious to her desperate struggles.

Chaff.

Wells rushed over and joined her effort to pry his fingers away from her neck, fighting against that delirium-strengthened grip. Maeko saw flashes of light in her vision, the blood trapped in her head started pounding in her ears. Tears welled in her eyes, both from physical pain and from heartache. Then Chaff sagged suddenly. The hand loosened and fell away as if the effort had become too much for him. He sank back to the table with a groan, his eyes slipping closed.

Wells was panting. "I'd say that arm works fine."

Maeko put a hand to her throat and backed away until she bumped into the wall. She felt the tears burning in her eyes.

Wells reached out to touch her forearm lightly. "Don't take it personal. I'm sure he's wanted to kill every person he's seen since they brought him here. I doubt he even recognized you with the fever and all the drugs in his system."

This is my fault. How could Chaff not hate her after what she'd brought him to?

"Are you sure?"

Wells didn't answer. He handed her the satchel. She took it and stood back out of the way while he released the final strap. When they were all off, he shook Chaff's shoulder gently, standing back far enough to leap out of the way if the lanky street rat attacked again.

Chaff mumbled something incoherent his eyes opening a small fraction. Wells crouched next to the bed and worked his arm around under Chaff's shoulder on the good side, slowly propping him upright.

"C'mon. We're going to get you out of here."

Chaff's eyes opened more at that, focusing a little. He nodded, though it was more of a wobbly bobbing of his head than an actual nod.

Wells lifted then, grimacing with the effort.

For a moment, the lean officer was forced to carry all of Chaff's weight, half-dragging him the first several steps, then Chaff managed to get his feet under him. They were about the same height, though Chaff had lost a fair bit of weight in the short time since she'd last seen him. Well's started toward the door, Chaff leaning heavily on him. His feet scuffed across the floor, his steps slow and uncoordinated. Maeko followed behind, staying out of Chaff's line of sight for the time being, just in case.

How would they ever get him up to the rooftop? How would they get him into the ship?

One thing at a time. "They're picking us up on the roof of the next building over. Is there another way to get up there? He isn't going to make it up the ladder like this."

Chaff lost his footing and Wells stumbled, crashing into the wall to catch himself. He leaned there for a moment, supporting Chaff while the lean street rat struggled to get his feet under him again.

"There's a stairwell inside the other building that will get us up to the roof. There's not much going on in that building yet so they assigned me duty there as one of the newer officers to the facility. There is one other guard though. I told him I was going to get some food in the commissary when I left."

"Can we get past him?"

Wells pushed away from the wall and resumed the slow trek. Chaff's breathing sounded strained, far more so than that of the officer trying to support him.

"I don't see that we have much choice," Wells muttered.

Maeko moved in front so she could sneak out and make sure the area was clear. Chaff didn't look at her. His eyes were mostly closed, all of his energy focused into making his feet move.

The slow trek between the buildings set her nerves on fire again. Not only did their sluggish pace increase the risk of being spotted, but it also ate up time they didn't have. They had to get to the airship within an hour, and it felt as if several had crawled by already.

Maeko opened the door to the adjacent building and peeked in. No sign of the other guard. She held the door for Wells and Chaff, then went ahead of them again, staying close enough to look back at Wells for directions whenever they reached a branch in the corridor.

"The stairwell is just around the corner at the end of this hall," Wells whispered as they rounded the third corner.

So close.

They'd made it about halfway down the hall when a door opened in front of them and Officer Tagmet stepped into their path. He leveled his gun at her head.

CHAPTER ELEVEN

I'm more than a bit disappointed in you, Wells."

Maeko stared down the gun barrel, a view she'd hoped to never have again, and yet, it kept happening to her. The price of all the risks she'd been taking. Maybe Chaff and Ash had a point there.

Wells was armed, but he would have to drop Chaff to get to his gun, and the mere act of doing so would give Tagmet plenty of warning as would any attempt by her to run for it.

"Don't give me that," Wells looked at Tagmet, his voice steady but laced with burning fury.

Maeko didn't think she'd ever heard the younger officer sound quite so angry and Tagmet's startled look suggested that he hadn't either.

Wells spoke again, taking advantage of the moment of surprise. "It's the Literati you should be disappointed in. Look at what they're doing here, Tagmet. Look at what they were doing to this boy."

Tagmet's eyes shifted to look over her shoulder at the two behind her. "He's a bloody Pirate and a kidsman. He's getting what he deserves."

Fresh rage welled in her. Could she move fast enough to shove his arm away before he fired on them? Did she have the conviction to shoot him if she could get his gun away?

Wells grunted behind her, perhaps shifting Chaff's weight. "He's not a Pirate and even if he were, no one deserves to be tortured like this. They were letting the infection slowly kill him. Can you even begin to imagine the pain he's going through?"

Tagmet's finger lifted from the trigger just a little and Maeko hesitated. Did the angry officer actually have a conscience?

"I can't just step aside and let you walk out of here. They'd have my head."

Crimson stepped around the corner behind Tagmet without a sound, her gun in hand. Wells had to see her too. Maeko kept her eyes on Tagmet's gun, determined not to betray the woman's presence.

"Yes," Wells countered. "You can let us go. Better yet, you can come with us."

Maeko bristled at the idea of Tagmet joining them. Fortunately, so did Tagmet.

"I'm not throwing in my lot with a bunch of Pirates and street rats. But…" He drew a ragged breath. "…I can't say you're entirely wrong."

He lowered the gun and Crimson paused, no more than a foot behind him now.

"If someone was to bludgeon me from behind though, I could tell them I never saw it coming." He met Maeko's eyes then and she realized that, somehow, he knew Crimson was there. "Mind you, I'd prefer if you try not to do any real damage."

Crimson met her eyes as well, looking a little disappointed at the failed stealth. Then she shrugged, flipped her pistol and used the grip to strike him behind the ear. Tagmet crumpled.

She stepped around him and hurried over to help Wells with Chaff. "Let's get moving. I didn't hit him that hard. He shouldn't be out long."

"How did you…?"

Crimson glanced at Maeko. "I saw you three enter this building from the rooftop and came down to help. Run upstairs. Ash should be dropping into range any minute. When he does, climb up and tell him to bring the ship down to the roof. Your friend is barely conscious enough to walk, let alone climb a rope ladder."

Maeko nodded and turned, sprinting around the corner and up the stairwell. She burst out through a door and onto the roof in the pouring rain. The ladder was there, hanging probably longer than it should have given no one had been there to signal Ash. Running to it, she grabbed the lower rung and yanked hard three times, then she pulled herself up and started to climb.

The slippery surface made for a miserable ascent, but she wrapped her arms and legs around the side and went as fast as she could. She was gasping for breath when she felt Ash reach down and grab her arm. He hauled her in and she stumbled into him, grabbing his shoulders for balance. His arms went around her, squeezing her tight for a few seconds before releasing her.

"You made it back." The front of his shirt was now wet from hugging her.

Her chest tightened. He wouldn't be so happy when she told him about his father.

"We have to drop down to the roof. Chaff can't climb."

Ash bobbed his head in affirmation and went to the controls. Maeko crouched down and began to pull in the ladder. Her arms were tired from the climb, but it needed doing and it kept her from fretting. It was risky dropping down, but they still had the heavy rain and dark to hide them. If they were quick, they could get down, pick the others up and set off again before anyone noticed. She got the ladder in and tucked away just as they reached the roof.

Crimson and Wells staggered in with Chaff, barely aware, supported between them. They made a quick decision and lowered him down in a corner instead of risking him falling out of one of the chairs. He slumped against the wall, his eyes sliding shut.

Ash gave Chaff's arm a startled look, then he turned to stare at the hatch. His look of confusion wrenched at Maeko's heart. Crimson went to the controls and Wells reached to pull the hatch shut. Ash grabbed his arm.

"Where's my dad?"

Wells met Maeko's eyes, but she couldn't find her voice to answer. Ash turned to face her, his features slack with dread. Wells jerked the hatch shut and turned the handle to latch it.

"We couldn't get to him, but he's okay," Maeko finally said. "He's doing engineering work for them. They're not going to hurt him."

Now his face flushed. "I don't bloody well care if they're going to hurt him. We have to get him out."

Ash spun and charged at Crimson who was taking the ship back up. Wells dove for him and the two slammed to the floor together. Ash aimed a kick at Wells's side, but the officer deflected it reflexively.

Wells blocked Ash's next punch and grabbed his wrist. He twisted the younger boy's arm back and forced him to the ground, pinning him there with a knee in his back. There was the clatter of handcuffs, then Wells got up, dragging a cuffed Ash up with him.

"Your father is beyond our reach. All of us would end up in their hands if we tried to get to him now. I'm sorry. As soon as you calm down," he nodded to the cuffs, "I'll take those off."

Ash turned away from Maeko and stepped over to drop into one of the chairs, his posture rigid and forward because of the cuffs binding his wrists behind him. In the sudden silence, the whir and click of Macak's leg became the loudest sound. The cat trotted across the floor of the gondola to where Chaff sat, his head back against the wall, his eyes still closed, breathing shallow. Macak rubbed against his healthy hand and he jerked, moving the hand into his lap. Not one to be discouraged, Macak circled around once and curled against his hip. Chaff's eyes flickered open, then his head turned away from them and the cat and he closed his eyes again. A few seconds later, his hand sank down to rest on Macak's warm back.

What could she do? She couldn't bring Ash his father back. She couldn't undo the injury that had been done to Chaff, the suffering he'd gone through and the pain still in store for him with treatment of the infected appendage. Fresh tears stung her eyes and she closed them. She started to sink to the floor and someone's hands clasped tight on her upper arms. Wells guided her to a chair then crouched down next to her.

"At least it was his left hand," he said in a hushed

voice.

Maeko didn't open her eyes. She couldn't bear to look at any of them. "He's left-handed."

"Oh." Wells squeezed her shoulder once, at a loss for anything more to say.

She heard him walk away.

The engines engaged. They were high enough up now to make their escape.

Hanging her head, she curled her legs into the chair and a few tears slipped through, dropping onto her hands folded in her lap. She would have welcomed Macak's company, but the cat had decided that Chaff needed him the most. Perhaps he was right.

#

When they had left the estate, the grounds were dark with only a few lanterns lit outside some of the buildings. Now the entire place was lit up brighter than an evening market. Drake was going to be furious, but what could he do to them now that it was done? She couldn't believe he would hurt them, or not Crimson at least. She hoped some of Crimson's influence would ease the punishment for the rest of them.

"Land in the center courtyard. It'll be easiest and they already know we're coming. We need to get your friend some medical care immediately." Crimson sounded worried, but determined.

Ash had calmed enough that Wells had let him go and he had gone back to piloting with Crimson at his shoulder. He started the descent. They would have to drop all the way down to get Chaff out. As they sank down closer to the ground, men moved out towards the airship, some of them carrying the anchor ropes, others carrying brandished guns. The ship touched down and the men with the anchors went to work.

Maeko kept a wary eye on the guns as the men trained them on the door. "I guess Drake's pretty miffed."

Crimson gave her a cynical glance and went to help Wells lift Chaff, who sagged on them, moaning. A tremor of fear swept through Maeko. He was in bad shape. Crimson was right, he needed medical attention now.

"It's the pain," Wells offered, making a weak attempt to be reassuring.

When they exited the airship, the brandished guns remained trained upon them. Drake came storming out of the manor with Tomoe and Ash's mother close behind. His dark eyes flashed in the lamplight, his wolfish countenance looking more predatory than ever as the rain slicked down his black hair. He stopped a few yards away from them, putting up an arm to signal Tomoe and Julia to stay back. With a quick glance, he took in the five of them, his expression unreadable.

"You two," he singled out two of the men holding guns, "take the young man to Dr. Carrigan. Tomoe, you go with him."

He gave Maeko's mother a sharp look when she opened her mouth to protest and she stayed silent, nodding instead.

"You four," Drake gestured to four more armed men, "escort the officer to my study and lock the rest up. I'll deal with them later."

The glare he gave Crimson then might have killed a lesser person, but she held her head high and faced it full on.

Two men moved in to take Chaff from Wells and Crimson.

Maeko stepped forward.

"Wait."

Drake didn't even look at her.

"Wells, give him the supplies for Chaff."

Drake paused and held out a hand to the officer. Wells passed over the bundle of medical supplies. Drake in turn handed the bundle to Tomoe then turned and walked back into the manor, confident that his orders would be carried out.

A guard of armed men escorted them toward the house. Julia called out to Ash as they went past, but he didn't look at her. He didn't raise his head. For him, the mission had been a failure. She glanced back at the men helping Chaff. With the barely conscious street rat between them, their progress was slow. Macak followed them.

Tomoe glanced at Maeko, met her eyes for a second, and looked away. Maeko heaved a sigh and faced forward.

If only they had been able to get Garrett back. Then Ash would be happy and Drake might not be this angry. Instead, they had brought back a drugged, direly injured street rat who had seemed less than thrilled to see her, to put it lightly, and a Literati officer.

I only wanted to make it better.

She felt like weights were hung over her shoulders, trying to drag her down as she let the armed men prod her along.

Inside the house, they split into two groups, with a couple of men escorting Wells toward the stairs and the other two guiding them down another hallway. They stopped again halfway down and one of the men opened a door. It looked like a door to any other room, and the interior looked as elegant as any bedroom in the manor, albeit much more sparsely furnished. The door itself was three times thicker than any others she'd seen in the building and it had no knob on the inside. A luxury prison cell?

The man took Ash's arm and guided him inside. Then he shut the door and locked it behind him. They escorted Maeko and Crimson to another similar room several doors down. The same man unlocked the door and held it open for them.

"You two can stay in here."

Maeko didn't move. "Why does Ash have to be alone?"

"Because it wouldn't be proper to lock you ladies up in there with him. If you know what's good for you, you'll shut up and go inside. Don't brass the boss man off any more than you already have."

Crimson put a hand on her shoulder and pushed gently. Maeko relented, walking into the room. The door shut and the lock clicked behind them. She sank down on the bed and put her face in her hands.

"I'm sorry, Crimson." Her hands muffled her voice, but she didn't want to look into the woman's eyes. She couldn't. Not yet. "I mucked everything up."

Crimson sat next to her and put an arm around her shoulders. "Maybe it feels that way now, Kitten, but

Chaff will get the care he needs now. It wasn't all for naught. Besides, we all do daft things in the name of love."

For some reason, those words broke a dam inside her and she began to sob, deep sobs that hurt her throat. Crimson slid one slender arm around her shoulders and pulled her close, rocking her gently as the tears fell.

F or the next five days, no one spoke to them at all. They were delivered meals in the room and escorted to the nearest privy when necessary. Crimson remarked on the latter with surprise, having expected Drake would be angry enough to force them to use bedpans instead of the newly installed facilities. Maeko was underwhelmed with the little luxuries.

A guard tossed Macak into the room with them the morning after their return and Maeko called out insults at him for his rough handling of the cat until Crimson shushed her. Beyond that brief exchange, neither of them spoke much of the circumstances behind their shared captivity. Crimson taught her several card games using a deck they found in one drawer and they chatted about simple things. They spent most of a day discussing Maeko's methods for picking out promising marks in a crowd and another afternoon vanished while Crimson explained the finer points of airship manufacturing.

The rest of the time, Crimson alternated between pacing while muttering under her breath and sitting at the one desk in the room with her head in her hands. Maeko amused herself with rearranging the décor, staring out the barred window, or petting Macak and trying to think of something worthwhile to say to her fellow prisoner. Since the whole mess was her doing, everything she came up with to offer consolation sounded completely inadequate in her head, so she said nothing.

Evening on the fifth day, the door swung open and a tall dour looking guard with a gun stepped into the doorway. He gestured to Maeko with the crooking of a finger, and she stood. Crimson stood too, but the man shook his head, giving the woman a hard glower. Awkwardly avoiding Crimson's frustrated glance, Maeko walked across the room with a sense of marching to her death and followed the man out.

Another armed guard shut and locked the door, then fell into step behind her and they escorted her that way, like a dangerous criminal, to the familiar room on the second floor where Drake held his small private meetings. The two men stepped up to either side of the door and the first one gestured for her to enter.

With a knot in her throat, Maeko opened the door. Drake stood by the window, his back to her, his figure made dark by the light coming in, turning him into a shadow of himself. She stepped inside and the door shut behind her.

She waited quietly. Anything she started with was almost certainly going to heighten his ire. As with thieving, silence was the safest option here.

He didn't move or acknowledge her in any way. Perhaps he meant for her to begin the conversation, forcing her to risk heightening his anger. Not entirely fair, since she'd had no warning and his insistence on looking away gave her no visual cues to work with, but it would do her no good in the long run to let him intimidate her.

She swallowed, lifted her chin, and took a few steps closer to the desk between them.

"You should forgive Crimson. She only went along with us because she didn't want us or your airship getting hurt." She added the airship on the logical assumption it might mean more to him than they did and that, therefore, Crimson acting in its defense might carry more weight.

His shoulders tensed. "She should have told me what you were planning in the first place. It never should have gotten that far."

The dangerous edge in his tone almost convinced her to let it go at that. Almost. But the whole mess had been her idea. That made it her fault, with no little complicity from Ash, but she wasn't going to let Crimson take the fall for their behavior.

"I never told her my plan. She caught us when we were already taking off in the airship. It was too late for her to do anything…" She trailed off when he snapped one hand up by his side.

"She still could have stopped you. She was armed. She should have forced you to land the airship and brought you to me. Then I could have seen to it that you didn't get another chance to attempt your foolish rescue." He turned and gave her a warning look that made her hold her tongue. He looked every bit the wolfish rogue she'd thought him to be when they first met and she suddenly wasn't as keen to test his temper. "Fortunately for you, your Literati friend has given us a great deal of useful information about the experiments and weapons development going on at that facility. If not for his willingness to cooperate, the whole venture would have been a colossal failure."

There was a painful throb in her chest. Longing. Sorrow. Guilt. At the peak of it all, anger that he would consider saving Chaff a failure. A flood of emotion she didn't know how to manage. She licked her lips and made herself meet his dark eyes.

"How is Chaff?" The question came out as something of a growl.

He gave her a long measuring look, letting her sweat for a minute as worry quickly overwhelmed her anger.

"The Lits weren't very kind to him, perhaps because his survival wasn't all that important if he didn't have any information to offer them. Gangrene had set into the wound and the infection was spreading fast. We had to amputate the arm to save him."

Maeko's stomach turned and she had to swallow bile.

Drake held up a hand again to stay any questions. "We've already modified one of the prosthetics we were working on to fit him. One much like mine with a few special features he should appreciate once he's healed. The recovery should go well for him now and use of the arm should be relatively painless once things are a little more healed, but he hasn't been very communicative. Some of that is the morphine. The amount they had him on was dangerously high and he is reacting poorly to having it reduced, but there's a lot of emotional anguish there as well." The corner of Drake's mouth twitched with a hint of a bitter smirk as if to say that emotional anguish was her problem, not his. "He isn't much use to us in his current state, so I thought I might send you to talk to him when we're done here, see if you can make any progress."

Did that mean he wasn't locking her up again? She would almost prefer the fancy prison cell to facing Chaff right then knowing the extent of the trauma she'd brought upon him.

"Don't think my letting you out means your extremely reckless behavior has been forgiven. The simple facts are that I need your assistance with more than just your ailing friend. Crimson had planned to send you to meet with Detective Emeraude later this week, so I need you involved in our planning."

"Me?"

He nodded. "Yes. She told me when you arrived at their last meeting the detective seemed to respect you."

"I'm not sure that's the most accurate observation."

He tapped the desk with his fingernails. A wry smirk twisted his lips. "Emeraude is a difficult woman to deal with, but Crimson is adept at reading people. If she says the detective respects you, I will trust in that. I can't throw someone she doesn't know into the mix and expect that woman to go along with it, so I don't see that I have much choice. I need to trust you although you have quite frankly given me little reason to. To ease my own mind, I will send two of my most trusted men with you to keep you out of trouble this time. If you try anything rash, they have my permission to use whatever force necessary to keep you in line."

Drake turned his back on her then and she stuck her tongue out at him.

"I'll pretend I didn't see that."

She flushed. Of course, the window glass would have reflected her image just fine.

"The gentlemen outside the door will escort you to your friend."

She didn't move. "You should let Crimson out."

"I'm going to. I need her working on my battleship."

She blew out a huff. "That's not enough. You need to forgive her too. She loves you."

"I know," he murmured as though speaking more to himself.

After perhaps a minute more of silence, she concluded that they were done and went to the door. There wasn't much more she could do for Crimson and no amount of delay was going to make talking to Chaff any easier.

The guards still didn't speak to her when she stepped out. The first man simply turned away and started walking. The second gestured for her to follow the first and fell into step behind her. Her gut twisted in knots while they walked, as if some malicious creature were living in there, trying to tear her apart from within. She clung to that thought, hoping the grossness of it would distract her from what waited, but with every step, she remembered his hand closing on her throat. The bruises there throbbed with the memory and her chest ached with a less tangible kind of pain.

He didn't realize it was me. Chaff would never hurt me.

The thoughts lacked conviction. He had every right to be angry with her. To hate her, even. He'd tried to talk her out of getting involved with the Pirates. In the end, she'd refused to let it go and he'd stayed by her because he cared about her only to end up like this, mutilated and remade against his will. Did he regret his decision to stay with her now? How could he not?

The first guard stopped outside a door and pulled a ring of keys from his pocket. Her nerves twittered like a flock of peeved birds. She twisted her hands together. It seemed to take forever for him to find the right one and the jangling of the keys as he flipped through them seemed absurdly loud. It was all she could do not to grab the ring from him and start trying them herself.

Finally, he selected a key, pushed it into the lock and turned. The click of the mechanism swept her back to the moment when she and Chaff had gone to try breaking Ash's brother out of the Literati orphanage. The way he had deferred to her skill in lock picking. The way their hands had touched upon the door handle. The spark of merry mischief in his blue eyes and the unexpected fondness in his smile.

She tried to swallow the painful lump forming in her throat. It didn't work.

The guard opened the door just enough for her to enter and stepped aside. She leaned in. The interior was dark. Curtains drawn over all the windows masked the undoubtedly bright and ornate interior with deep shadows. Her feet were stuck to the floor, refusing to move into the room.

The other guard put a hand on her shoulder and put a little pressure there. Her hackles went up when he touched her, not only with his nerve at feeling he had the right to do so, but also with her own cowardice. She moved out from under his hand and into the dim interior. The door closed behind her, taking away the light that came in from the hallway.

She stood there for a moment, letting her eyes adjust until she could make out the long, lean figure stretched on the bed with his back to the door. Delaying a little longer, she searched out the knob on the gas light next to the door and turned it, chasing back the shadows with flickering light.

That light reflected off the metal arm attached at his shoulder, dancing upon its cold, unyielding surface. His torso was bare, revealing leather straps around his lean frame that helped support the mechanism. She stared at the prosthesis, trying to swallow around the lump in her throat and fighting the temptation to turn the light off again and leave.

He didn't move. Perhaps he was asleep and he probably needed the sleep after all he'd been through. She would come back later.

She started to turn toward the door.

"What do you want?"

The bitter tone didn't do much for her confidence. She opened her mouth to answer, but no words came out. What did she want? What did Drake think she could do here?

"Unless you're bringing something for the pain, I'd rather you buggered off."

"Chaff?"

His entire body tensed as if he'd received an electric shock. "Maeko?"

No teasing mispronunciation of her name. No annoying nicknames. She took a few steps toward the bed, her gut squirming. "Yes."

"Leave me alone." His voice sounded tight now.

Her chest tightened in response. She reversed her steps and turned to the door, lifting her hand to knock for the guards to let her out, but her hand hovered a few inches from the door then sank back to her side. If it was possible to make this better, it wasn't going to be through giving up and walking away.

Still facing the door, she said softly, "You've always taken care of me. Let me take care of you this time."

"Feeling guilty, Pigeon?" His tone was sharp, meant to cut her. "Don't you think you've done enough already?"

The words tore through her like a mess of flung daggers. She turned. He was sitting up on the bed now, facing her. His bare chest showed off the collection of scars from a lifetime surviving on the streets. She'd witnessed the making of many of those scars, more than one the result of him coming to her defense. The arm was the one injury she couldn't quite come to terms with.

Did she feel guilty?

Yes. Very much so.

"I never meant for this to happen."

"Get out." His bloodshot eyes bored into her. His face was a pallid impenetrable mask. More than unfriendly, but she could see pain behind the hostility in his eyes, an all-consuming misery that she yearned to fix. "I don't want to see you. Not now. Not ever."

There was snapping sensation inside her, as if something broke apart with his words. That something fell away, revealing a desolate, hollow space inside. She didn't realize she was moving back again until her heel bumped into the door. The door opened, the guard apparently mistaking her impact for a knock, and she stumbled back out into the hallway. The guard shut the door, cutting off her view of those eyes.

"Maeko."

She turned.

Ash's mother, Julia, was across the wide hall, stopping mid-stride to look askance at her. Ash was beside her, his pale green eyes hard and cold as Chaff's had been when he looked at Maeko, still resenting that they had rescued Chaff and not his father. He held her gaze for a few seconds then his focus moved past her to the door. His jaw tightened, his lips pressing into a bitter line. He turned and walked away.

The hollow inside deepened and filled with ice.

Maeko pulled her shoulders back and walked down the hall away from Chaff's room and in the opposite direction from Ash. The guards didn't follow this time. She walked to the back of the manor and opened a door to the rear gardens. As soon as she stepped through the door, it began to rain, going from no precipitation to downpour in a few seconds. That was fine with her. It would hide the tears.

A few horses in one of the rear pastures trotted out to shelter under a stand of trees. She walked to the fence and stared out at them. They stared back, their ears perked, but they weren't willing to venture into the heavy rain to investigate. Eventually, they lost interest, turning to grazing the sparse grass beneath the trees. She sank to her knees in the wet grass at the edge of the fence and let the rain wash her hair into her face, let the water run together with the tears, let the cold outside soak into her skin to merge with the new cold place at her core.

Everything she did, no matter how good her intentions, turned out wrong. Perhaps she needed to leave this place. She could go back to the streets where she belonged.

Except she didn't feel like she belonged there, not without Chaff. He had been her family for so much of her life. Her one constant friend and companion, even in her darkest moments. Until now.

Her mother was here, but their relationship was tenuous at best. Years of abandonment didn't go away with a few heartfelt chinwags. There was no good reason to stay here and nowhere else to go. Nowhere to go and no one to go with.

Someone walked up behind her and the rain stopped hitting her, pattering instead on the fabric of the umbrella they held out over her head.

"Come inside, Kitten," Crimson urged. "If not for your sake then for Macak's. The poor creature has been yowling at the door for the better part of an hour wanting to come see you regardless of the rain."

"I don't deserve him," she muttered.

"Oh, bollocks," Crimson snapped. "Get off your arse and get inside or I'll drag you there myself."

Maeko stood, shivering with cold, and let Crimson lead her back into the manor where Macak was indeed waiting at the door. He hopped up on a side table and up to her shoulders as she walked past, his claws digging in through her wet clothes while he got his balance. The pain was sharp. Welcome. She felt a fraction less alone as he pushed his head against her cheek. Perhaps only a cat-sized fraction less alone, but it was a start.

Maeko hid away in an upstairs corner sitting room for much of the next few days, a quiet room used so rarely that sheets covered most of the furniture to keep the dust off. It was enough for her to know that Crimson and Ash weren't locked up anymore. She didn't need to talk to them or to anyone. Besides, it was painfully clear that Chaff didn't want to talk to her and Ash didn't seem interested in her company either. She refused to talk to Crimson beyond asking that the woman leave her alone and not tell anyone where she was. Crimson insisted on bringing her food now and then, but consented to leave her with only Macak for company outside of that.

It wasn't so hard to appreciate the affection the cat gave her. The purring warm ball of black and white fur with his one metal leg was her solitary success. She'd kept him out of Thaddeus's hands at the very least. There was very little doubt that the horrible man would have treated him badly. After all, Thaddeus had murdered his own brother. She didn't see him extending any great kindness to a cat.

Then again, Thaddeus wasn't likely to do much worse than his brother had by amputating the poor cat's leg to experiment with the false appendage in the first place.

And there was the rub. After everything she'd done to help Lucian Folesworth, after coming to trust and even like the seemingly kind and generous man, he had turned out to be no better than the rest of them. Perhaps his cruelty had a nobler purpose in trying to help people like Captain Garrett's younger son who'd lost a leg in an accident. Did that make it all right to torture another living being?

She stared at the gleaming metal leg with its elegant engravings while she stroked Macak's fur, trying to recapture the fascination the device held for her the first time she saw it in that grimy alleyway. The wonder was gone, replaced by upsetting disgust for the cruelty that led to him having the thing.

Was there nothing good in this world?

Macak purred and shifted, wrapping one fuzzy paw over his eyes. One ear twitched as he drifted on the edge of sleep in her cat-warmed lap.

Lucian was dead. Macak had adjusted to his modification, even if it had been unnecessary. Perhaps she needed to adjust to her situation as well.

Would Chaff adjust to his?

Macak made a small sound of protest and she quickly opened the hand that had begun clenching on his fur. His big eyes regarded her for a moment, perhaps deciding if she could be trusted not to commit the infraction again, then he settled once more and she stroked him in gentle apology.

Her thoughts turned to the battleship under construction in Drakes underground workshop. A device built for destruction. Would they also use the schematics she'd stolen from Lucian's flat to build weapons as Thaddeus was doing? More misery that she'd helped make possible. How many innocents would pay with their lives for this war between the Literati and the Pirates? What price was too high?

She tasted the coppery tang of blood and realized she'd been chewing on her lip too hard. The pain was crisp, refreshing. Something other than the icy hollow in her chest for her to focus on.

Was there a way to stop this madness? Could the Bobbies do something? Maybe meeting with Em was an opportunity. She couldn't make the past mistakes right, but maybe she could help stop this thing before it got worse. If the Bobbies knew what was going on at the new Literati prison, mightn't they intervene?

She startled when the door opened and Crimson entered with a plate of food. Her mouth flooded with saliva, and her stomach growled loud enough that Crimson smirked as she set the plate on the small table next to her.

"Want some company while you eat, Kitten?"

"No."

The amused smirk faded. "You can't take on the world all alone."

She looked down at her lap where Macak had lifted his head to peer with wide-eyed interest at the contents of the plate. He sniffed the air.

"I'm not."

Crimson pursed her lips and sat in another chair. "Macak is a wonderful companion, but you need more than a cat in your life."

Maeko picked up the fork and transferred a bite of game hen to her mouth to avoid having to say anything.

While she chewed, she pulled off another piece and offered it to Macak who made short work of it and glanced up at her in hope for more. She couldn't stop a grin, knowing that if she looked away for a moment he would steal what he was so politely asking for while he had her attention.

It'd been a while since she'd had to go hungry or even find food for herself. It was a nice way to live. One she should avoid getting too comfortable with. Whatever happened from this point, it was becoming clear that she didn't belong here.

"Emeraude's talking with the Bobbies to convince them to investigate Mr. Folesworth in connection with the commissioner's murder and the airship explosion, but Drake doesn't want them getting involved in things too deeply yet. He's afraid they'll tie things up with their politics and procedures and Thaddeus will have more than enough time to develop his weapons and start wiping out the Pirates. According to your Officer Wells, the new Literati prison is a development and testing ground for numerous weapons including a variety of modified prosthetic limbs intended to transform prisoners into deadly Literati soldiers."

Maeko thought of the dead bludger with the crude false arm who had attacked her—and of Drake's far more refined mechanical arm with its hidden gun. What would happen if they began equipping prisoners with such things and putting them to work for the Lits? Would the prisoners really work for them or would they just go rogue and start killing whomever they pleased? How could the Lits hope to control men who had already proven their willingness to break the law?

She began to feel nauseous, but she made herself keep eating so she wouldn't have to say anything, passing more nibbles of game hen to a very appreciative Macak as she ate.

"Drake is pushing us to finish the battleship faster so he can use it to attack the facility and put an end to the development."

"But…" Maeko swallowed the suddenly tasteless mouthful of food when Crimson frowned at her for starting to speak with her mouthful. She choked it down around a rising sense of alarm before continuing. "There are innocent people there too, like Captain Garrett."

"He knows that. We all know that, but the number of people who stand to suffer if they aren't stopped quickly is far greater."

"So, you think Drake's making the right decision?"

Crimson didn't answer. She stared out the window, her jaw clenching and unclenching fretfully. The light coming in from outside backlit her profile, emphasizing her strong nose. Somehow, it made her look more fiercely beautiful. A woman ready to take on the opposition using whatever means necessary.

"There must be another way." Maeko prompted.

"I don't know, Kitten. I see his point. We might be better off to take action now and deal with the consequences. The Bobbies are going to follow procedure and, right now, they're far from convinced that the wrong Mr. Folesworth survived the airship explosion. By the time they're ready to make any move against him, assuming they ever get to that point, we'll all be holding up stones."

Maeko winced inwardly. Holding up a stone was Chaff's favorite slang for death. She didn't want to think about him right now with his bloodshot eyes and broken body. "Why bother meeting with Em at all if we're not going to work with the Bobbies?"

"Anything we can give her now to help push them toward doubting Mr. Folesworth and beginning an investigation will only serve our cause in the aftermath. I can't talk Drake out of this, but maybe we can find a way to keep him out of prison once the dust settles."

Maeko sneered. "He refused to help me. Why should I help him?"

"He refused because he didn't want anyone put needlessly at risk and you turned around and stole his airship."

"You helped us. And it isn't like he didn't get the blasted thing back unharmed. Bloody dodger." She growled the last convincingly enough that it startled Macak who leapt from her lap and scurried under a chair in the corner. His departure lent potency to the hollow inside her and she drew in a deep breath, trying to fill the gap with something.

Crimson stared after the cat, green eyes flashing with anger. Her slender fingers gripped the arms of her chair.

Maeko braced for the verbal lashing she saw lurking behind the irked expression, but it didn't come. In the silence, Macak crept out from under the chair and walked toward Crimson, his steps tentative. Just out of her reach, he stopped and offered an inquisitive meow, his ears flicking forward hopefully. Crimson's hands slowly relaxed. Macak jumped up in her lap and her eyes softened as he arched into the hand she ran over his back.

Cat magic.

Despite a twinge of jealousy, Maeko appreciated the way he'd deflected the woman's anger. There were enough people upset with her. It wasn't productive to add more to the list.

She picked at her meal in cautious silence while Crimson relented to Macak's insistent prodding for affection.

"Will you at least talk to Em? See what you can do to get the Bobbies on the right track to exposing Thaddeus while still keeping them out of our way long enough to take him and his Literati cohort down. Pirates and innocent folks are dying on the streets every week now in clashes with the Lits. It won't be long before it's a daily occurrence. Do this for me and for your mother and all of the other people whose lives are at risk if their weapons development isn't stopped."

And who's going to stop Drake? Maeko blinked at the sudden stinging in her eyes and nodded, not trusting herself to speak. A cloak of dread landed heavy on her shoulders with the gesture.

"Thank you, Kitten. I owe you one. Your escorts will come for you tomorrow evening and take you into the city to meet with her."

My guards. Maeko pushed around the rest of the food on her plate and said nothing.

Crimson stroked the cat for a few silent minutes more, then she pushed him gently off and went to the door. Macak moved over to Maeko's lap, her earlier infraction upon his calm already forgiven.

"Oh," Crimson paused with her hand on the door handle. "Someone else wanted to talk to you."

She opened the door then and Maeko saw her mother waiting there. Her chest tightened, but she said nothing as the two women traded places. She focused on stroking Macak, making amends. The cat was happy to curl back down in her lap.

Tomoe entered the room and sat in the chair Crimson had vacated only a moment ago. Maeko found herself wondering if the seat was still warm.

The door had barely clicked shut when she spoke. "You are going out again tomorrow? To help them?"

Maeko nodded, once more finding that she didn't quite trust herself to speak.

"You should know that I think you are very brave. The things you have done to help the Pirates, to help Ash and his family, to rescue your friend..."

"Chaff," she offered.

"Yes."

She folded her fine hands in her lap as she often did and gazed at Macak, a soft, sad smile curving her lips, pulling on some of her scars. Maeko marveled at how she was still so beautiful and somehow put off such an air of serenity in defiance of her scars.

Macak butted his head into Maeko's palm. His purr was loud in the silence.

"How he loves you," Tomoe murmured, smiling at the cat, then she looked at Maeko. "How I love you."

A tear came from nowhere and slid down Maeko's cheek, she swallowed against the sudden sting in her throat.

"You are remarkable, Mae. You are strong and

brave and sometimes foolhardy, but so often in an effort to protect those you care for. I wish I would have been there for you, but I do not believe I could have done better than you have done for yourself. I think you should know that I am very proud of you."

More tears streamed down Maeko's cheeks now. Almost as though he knew what she was going to do before she did, Macak pushed into her hand once more then hopped down from her lap. She got up from her chair and Tomoe stood with her. Maeko stepped into her mother's open arms and buried her face in her clothes, squeezing her eyes shut.

"I love you, Mum," she choked out. "I'm sorry… for everything."

Tomoe's arms closed around her, providing a sense of comfort and safety she almost felt guilty indulging in.

"You have nothing to apologize for. I should never have considered letting you go. I have always loved you, Mae, and I always will."

#

They would be coming to get her soon to leave for the city. That sense of dread that had come over her when she agreed to meet Em had only intensified. Her meeting with her mother had healed some more wounds, but had somehow made the feeling worse, as though she were reconciling before leaving. It had also prompted her to this place, standing outside of the door to Chaff's room. She'd tried to catch Ash as well, but no one seemed to know where he'd gotten off to. Now she reached for the door with Macak draped over her shoulders and two expressionless guards staring on.

A large part of her wanted to simply go. She could

deal with this when she got back from the city. Still, that sense of dread prodded her on. It needed to be now. There were things that needed saying and there was no time like the present. She told herself that it was simply because talking to him now would limit the conversation and they would both have time to think about things while she was in town. That didn't feel like the truth though. It felt, again, like reconciling before saying goodbye.

The room was dark, but this time, when she lit the gas lamp, Chaff was standing by a window staring out. His face was drawn, with pain perhaps, or some deeper distress. His color was better though. He was healing. Recovering from the treatment of the Lits and the surgery. He didn't look at her when she came in. Instead, he gazed down at the metal hand of the prosthesis and closed it into a fist.

"Are you feeling better?" The words came out with a tremor.

"Why are you here?"

She swallowed and said, "I wanted to see you."

His lip tightened in a bitter smirk as he held out his arms to either side. "Well, have a look at me? I'm a scarred, disfigured street rat. A freak. I'm nothing."

She drew a deep breath, taking a little comfort from the cat on her shoulders, and barreled ahead. "Yes, Chaff, I have looked at you. I've looked at you a lot lately, in ways I never expected to look at you, and you know what I see. I see someone I love. I see someone who has risked himself time and time again to protect me. I see someone who has been an integral part of my past. A person who helped me become who I am now. I see someone I want in my life, now and always."

He stood there, staring at the hand. Opening and closing it. He was turned away enough that she couldn't quite read his expression. He said nothing.

"Thank you for everything you have ever done for me."

He still said nothing.

"I love you. That's all." She swallowed the tightness in her throat and turned. Would he speak now?

She grabbed the door handle.

Now?

She opened the door.

Nothing.

She stepped through and shut it behind her.

E m leaned in the door of the coach, the men's bowler hat she wore pulled low on her brow, shadowing her eyes. Adding the hat with the long frock coat and her short hair, she could almost pass as a slender man. She glanced at Maeko and then gave a hard look to the two guards. "What's this about?"

"Just a formality, Miss," one of the men replied.

"Tell Drake he can shove his formality up his arse for all I care. I'm not talking to her with you two bludgers in here. If he doesn't trust me, he doesn't need to work with me."

Em spun on her heel and started to walk away.

Maeko clutched Macak to her chest with one hand and popped up from the seat. One of the guards threw an arm out between her and the door and she gave him a withering look before calling after the detective.

"Wait!"

Em stopped and stood facing away from them, indecisive. Her hand fiddled with the clip on her holster.

Maeko was probably going to regret saying this, but she wasn't going to let the trip into town be wasted. "The guards aren't here for you. They're here to keep me out of trouble."

Several seconds followed in silence. The dark of the

129

nighttime street wrapped around them. Fog crept up the side streets, rolling in off the river, promising to smother the city in its pungent embrace.

Em started to laugh. She laughed hard enough that she bent over and snorted several times. Maeko plopped back down on the seat and glared at the guard across from her whose lips twitched with the effort of not smiling. She was sorely tempted to knock on the roof and signal the coachman to leave, but she had an important task, so she stayed put, grinding her teeth and waiting for Em to control her mirth.

After a minute or two, Em regained her composure and walked back up to the coach. Her eyes glinted with knife edged humor. "I can't imagine why they'd be worried about a sweet little bird like you getting into trouble. What'd you do to earn two burly nannies?"

Maeko gave her a sour look, refusing to dignify the comment with a reply. Macak squirmed and she eased her tightening grip on him.

Em considered the two men for a moment and smirked. "Since you blokes are just playing nursemaid, perhaps you wouldn't mind stepping outside and giving us a little privacy."

The men stiffened.

Maeko rolled her eyes. "Where can I possibly go?"

The two caught each other's eyes, then one nodded and Em stepped to the side as they climbed out. She climbed in behind them and shut the door firmly enough to make Macak jump in Maeko's arms.

"Where are Amos and Reuben?"

"Hiding out nearby watching the area. We're all being hunted right now. Especially you, Pigeon. It's best to practice some degree of caution. Why did you bring the bloody cat?"

Maeko shrugged, hating in that moment that Em had used the same nickname for her as Chaff did. As for Macak, the cat had moved up on her shoulders as soon as she let go and she'd thought nothing of having him there. In fact, she rather preferred it. If the opportunity to make a break came up, she wanted to take him with her, foolish as the notion probably was with nowhere to go and the fact that she was indeed being hunted. The first time out, however, her guards were likely to be too diligent. Perhaps, if this went well, the next time out they would grow careless. Assuming there was a next time out.

"I have to know. What did you do to make Drake feel that he needs to keep you under guard?"

The driving curiosity in Em's gray eyes told here they wouldn't get anywhere until they got this out of the way. "I borrowed his airship."

Em smirked again. "Borrowed without asking I presume."

Maeko scowled at the curtained window.

"And what did you need an airship for?"

"I used it to break Chaff out of the Lit prison."

Em's mouth dropped open in an uncharacteristic display of surprise. "You did what?"

"Broke Chaff out of the prison," she muttered, eager to move to another subject.

"You never cease to amaze me. With everything you've survived, you must be the luckiest rat in London, or the cleverest, but I'm not willing to give you that much credit just yet. It's almost a shame we aren't still working together, but I suppose Drake has more to offer."

Maeko set her jaw and stared at the woman across from her.

"All right. Seems you aren't up for talking about your escapades with your new comrades. Do you have any more information for me? I need to give the Metropolitan Police Service something if I'm going to convince them to open this investigation into Mr. Folesworth's death."

"No." Maeko swallowed. How far would Em go with her on this? How loyal was she to the Pirates she was working with? "They need to investigate all of that in time, but I think it's far more important that they investigate the new Literati prison facility and I want them to do it right away."

Em stared, her eyes boring into Maeko as if drilling for a deeper meaning behind the words. "*You* want? I take it by your choice of words that this isn't what Drake wants."

Macak's warm body curled around the back of her neck gave her the courage to keep going. "Drake is planning to attack the facility with the battleship he's building."

Em's eyes widened. Perhaps she hadn't known about the battleship. Now that Maeko thought about it, that wasn't too surprising if she had a tumultuous relationship with Drake.

"Thaddeus and the Lits are using the prison to run experiments on prisoners and develop dangerous weapons that they can use to take down the Pirate uprising. Drake wants to stop them before they can start using those weapons to round up the Pirates in the city."

Em licked her lips slowly. "Why didn't Crimson mention any of this?"

"Drake doesn't want the Bobbies interfering. He thinks they'll slow things down with their policies and procedures until it's too late to stop Thaddeus. Innocent people will die if he attacks that facility, but Thaddeus does need to be stopped before he can wage a full-on war against the Pirates in the city and kill even more innocents. You need to get the Bobbies to investigate that prison and shut down their operations before either of those things happen."

Em held up her hands and shook her head. "Hold on. This is an awful lot to dump on me. Why don't you start by telling me who's in that prison that you're trying to protect? You got your beau out. I don't buy that you just care about a bunch of guards and criminals that much."

"I don't want anyone to die needlessly, but yes, Captain Garrett is in there. They have him working on the weapons development, which means he's likely to be spending most of his time in the buildings Drake most wants to destroy."

Em rubbed her hands on her trousers as if trying to warm them. Her brow furrowed. "I'd say you were barmy, Pigeon, but I've seen a few things lately. A couple of strange blokes have been involved in Literati raids in Southwark the last two days. Big rough types, not the kind you want to run into on the street, each with a functional metal arm housing concealed weaponry. Remarkable appendages and disturbingly lethal. You just saved me a fair bit of risky detective work if what you say is true. But if Thaddeus and the Lits are going to the trouble to develop weapons that complex, I doubt shutting the Pirates up is the extent of their ambitions. They could be planning a coup on a much larger scale."

Em began to clasp and unclasp the strap on her holster, her focus turning inward. Maeko waited quietly, scratching Macak's head and letting the detective's brain work uninterrupted. After several minutes, those gray eyes focused in on Maeko with a gleam that made her entirely uncomfortable.

"If someone could get inside that facility…"

Maeko shook her head. "I got in there once, but I had an airship and inside help. I'm not planning to go back."

"Inside help?"

"Officer Wells."

Em drew back. "I would never have guessed him for a turncoat. Once again, I am impressed by your resourcefulness. I imagine you gave him that special look you use to get your way all the time."

Maeko felt her cheeks flush.

Em nodded. "I thought so. How much does he know about the prison?"

"Enough that he decided to switch sides."

Em chewed her lip in thought for a moment. "He must know a fair bit then. Can you get me in touch with him?"

"I could arrange to have him come along next time." Drake might go for it if she explained how much Wells knew about the events leading up to Lucian Folesworth's murder.

"Perfect. Tomorrow night then."

Tomorrow. "I don't know if I can arrange it that fast."

"Figure it out, Pigeon. You always manage." Em reached for the door. "Remember those lives that are at stake."

"We could work together again," Maeko blurted.

Em sat back and raised her brows at Maeko. "Drake's hospitality not good enough for you?"

Maeko chewed at her lip a moment, weighing the warm meals and comfortable quarters against the intense misery of being around so many people who were either angry with her or simply didn't seem to understand her.

"I don't belong there."

Em's soft smile held unexpected sympathy. "I've always had trouble settling into society myself. Perhaps that's why I do what I do." She was silent for a long time, gazing at Macak as if some secret waited to be revealed in his half-lidded eyes. "Tell you what, Pigeon. Get me a chance to talk with Wells and I'll see what I can do about arranging a place for you to stay as my assistant, but you bloody well better expect to work for it."

Maeko nodded, solemn and determined. "I do."

Em opened the door and climbed out without bothering with any departing niceties and Maeko stared after her until the guards ducked back into the coach. What the woman lacked in social graces she made up for in her willingness to believe in Maeko. Maybe Crimson was right. Maybe there was some respect there after all and, perhaps, though she didn't dare hope for too much just yet, a future.

#

It was late when they returned and the manor was relatively quiet. Maeko's guards left her once she was inside with Macak settled happy on her shoulders again, his warm body pressed against her neck.

She stood staring at the sweeping staircase with its vine-like railing and the magnificent rearing stallion sculpture in the center of the entry for a long time. The manor was luxurious in a way that even Lucian's fancy flat in the Airship Tower couldn't begin to compare to. Living with Lucian had been nice for a brief time, but even there she had fast begun to get restless. Perhaps she simply wasn't made for this kind of life.

Her gaze wandered up the staircase and focused first on the hallway she knew led to Ash's room, then drifted toward the one that led to where they had Chaff locked up.

Was it worth trying to talk to either of them or should she just quietly gather her things and make her exit after the meeting with Em tomorrow? Would Em be ready to take her on that soon?

It didn't really matter. If the woman wasn't ready, then she would find a way to take care of herself and Macak until she was.

Movement on the second floor caught her eye, metal reflecting the light of a gas lamp further down one hallway. She stepped back into the deep shadow beneath the statue and put a hand on Macak's shoulders to keep him still. The cat froze, responding to the change in her bearing as much as her touch. A figure slipped through the shadows and down the stairs in near perfect silence.

Chaff.

She sunk back, putting the statue between them until his quiet steps moved away again. Leaning out, she spotted him sneaking toward a hall at the back of the entry that led to the rooms they had set up for medical supplies and tending urgent injuries. He was keeping to the deepest shadows, which made it rather plain that he wasn't supposed to be out and about. Bad on Drake for underestimating the street rat, but then, it wasn't a surprise given that he'd underestimated her more than once.

Chaff stopped at one of the doors, looked around once, forcing her to duck back into the shadows hastily, then he crept inside. Taking off her shoes, she padded to the room and put her ear to the doorjamb to listen. Soft rustling sounds came from within, the light chink of metal or glass objects bumping together, his unfamiliar metal hand perhaps causing trouble in what would normally be a silent process.

What are you after?

There was a sinking sensation in her gut before the thought even finished. Macak touched her cheek with his cold, damp nose and purred. She pushed down the lever to open the door, slow and silent, easing comfortably back into the familiar role of thief and pickpocket.

The low light of a barely burning gas lamp illuminated Chaff standing before a series of opened drawers and cupboards. He was so engrossed in what he was doing that he didn't notice her slipping inside and shutting the door just as silently behind her. He stood drawing something out of a bottle with a syringe with his good right hand, but when he went to switch the syringe to the metal hand, he fumbled, dropping it twice and cursing under his breath before she got up the nerve to speak.

"What are you doing?"

He jerked and spun around, striking one hip on an open drawer and cursing again as his lip curled in a pained grimace. He stared at her for a long moment, rubbing his hip with his good hand. His skin was pallid, glossed with a sheen of sweat, and his muscles vibrated with small spasms. After what felt like at least a minute of silent scrutiny, his eyes narrowed.

"Help me with this. I can't do it with this bloody arm."

She took a few steps closer. "Is that morphine?"

"They didn't give me enough today. I just need it for the pain."

"I'm sure the doc will help you. Why don't I go—"

"No!"

She took a step back. "I'm not doing it without talking to him first."

There was barely enough time to leap out of the way when he hurled the syringe at her head. Macak tried to hang on, his claws digging gouges in her flesh before he finally gave up and jumped clear. The syringe broke against the wall.

"This happened because of you," Chaff snarled, pointing to the false arm with his good hand. "The least you could do is help me deal with the pain. Bloody worthless twist."

She winced as he turned his back on her and began

digging through another cupboard. Then the sting of the cat scratches overcame the sting of his words and she stood up straight. Macak cowered under a chair, watching with big eyes as she strode partway across the room.

"I'm sorry about what happened. I really am." He froze with his right hand in the cupboard. "But this isn't you. The Chaff I know would be fighting this. He'd be learning how to use that arm and busting his arse to fight free of the drugs the Lits tried to drown him in. Look at yourself. Your better than this."

She gave that a few seconds to sink in then continued.

"You don't have to forgive me. That's fine." It wasn't really. She knew that by the feeling of raw pain in her throat when she said it, but she forced herself to keep talking. "But don't do this to yourself. Please."

Chaff's hand sank down slowly, coming to rest on the counter. "I taught you to survive. I protected you. I did everything I could to take care of you. I even let you go when that seemed to be what you wanted. When you came back, when Diggs and I saved you from that bludger, then I thought maybe you'd decided to stay, but I was never enough for you. The least you can do is give me enough consideration to let me go now."

She stared at his bare back. At the muscles and the scars. At where flesh ended and the false arm began. The scratches on her shoulder stung, blood seeping into the fabric of her shirt. She turned and went to the door. When she opened it, Macak scurried out around her feet.

"I loved you." His voice was soft, but clear.

Loved.

Maeko jerked the door shut on him, but the words hung in the air, heavy like the weight of the river closing over her head. He had saved her then too. He was right, he had done so much for her, and all she did was take advantage of his affection. There was little doubt that he would be better off without her there.

It was decided then. Tomorrow night she would go to meet Em again and she wouldn't come back.

There wasn't much to take. Most of the clothes she'd been wearing were borrowed, so she put on the boy's clothing Em had given her during their brief stint working together before Lucian's murder and slipped a set of lock picks into one boot. In the other, she concealed a slender knife she'd pick up from the weapons stash down near the medical area. There were no guns small enough that she felt confident trying to conceal one considering that Wells would be along for the ride.

The only thing she really regretted having to leave behind was Macak's carrying case. It would be safer for him in a lot of situations, but he liked riding on her shoulders and had done so often enough that bringing his case along would draw attention and they would know something was up.

"Are you ready?"

She turned to see Wells standing in the doorway, his hands tucked into his pockets and his shoulders hunched. The posture made him look a lot younger than he was, almost as young as Chaff and, without his Literati uniform, he looked a lot more approachable. He shifted from one foot to the other and she wondered passingly if she might be the cause of that discomfort or if it was just the challenge of adjusting to the new environment. He had switched sides rather dramatically after all and wasn't even close to being fully trusted by the Pirates.

She glanced at Macak and tapped her shoulder. The cat leapt up from the dresser and she clenched her teeth when he landed and began to knead over the top of the scratches from the night before.

"I'm ready."

"You're dressing like that?"

There was an almost disappointed edge in his voice and she gave him a sour look. "Yes. We're just meeting Em, not some royal dignitary."

Wells cracked a bemused grin.

"What?"

"If you only dress up for dignitaries, then I suppose I should be flattered."

Maeko exhaled exasperation and rolled her eyes as she slipped through the door past him. "Dignitaries and gullible officers," she muttered.

Wells only chuckled good-naturedly and gave the cat on her shoulders an odd smirk as they passed.

On the way to the coach, she spotted Ash working with the farrier to put shoes on a patient black mare. As she watched, the farrier finished a hoof and passed the tools to Ash, putting him to work on the next hoof. At least he'd found a productive way to spend his time when he wasn't down working on the airship. She hurried up into the waiting coach to get out of sight before he had an opportunity to spot her and give her another of those heartbreakingly cold looks.

The one guard Drake sent with them this time sat up with the driver. It was a bit insulting that he appeared to trust Wells more than he did her, but then, she had stolen his airship. The silence in the coach was deafening as they headed into the city. Macak stood on Maeko's thighs, staring at Wells expectantly while rising on his toes to push his back into her affectionate scratches. Every wobble made him dig his claws in, but she merely clenched her teeth and wondered how Wells had gained immunity to the power of cat eyes. It was a good twenty minutes before either of them spoke and she would have been happy enough to continue that way.

"You know what Drake's planning?"

Maeko met the officer's eyes for a second then focused on Macak who turned around suddenly and half-climbed her chest to push his head into her chin. She grinned and scratched his cheeks with both hands.

Wells tried again. "I'm sure he isn't telling the detective everything."

"What does it matter?"

The ex-officer's jaw tightened briefly. "He isn't telling me much either. I gave up everything to help you and the Pirates. I think I deserve a little honesty."

Maeko kissed the cat on the head, then lifted her shoulders in a slight shrug as he curled back down in her lap.

"You helped me do something I didn't have their approval to do. Then you took sanctuary with them," Maeko reminded him. "I don't know why you would expect Drake to tell you everything right away. You were a Lit officer. I think he's showing considerable trust letting you go to meet with Em like this."

He blew out and deflated visibly. "You're right. Blast if I don't hate needing a street rat to point out the obvious."

"A street rat and a twist at that," she added with a teasing smirk that almost sparked a little pleasure in the hollow inside her.

Wells shook his head at her comment. "You're more than you let on. There's a clever head on your shoulders. A rather fine looking one too, if you don't mind me saying."

"Don't start that," she growled, annoyed by the flush she felt rising in her cheeks.

Wells just chuckled, clearly enjoying her discomfort, but he was polite enough not to press it further, letting the ride lapse back into silence.

#

Though they hadn't discussed the need for prudence, Em was surprisingly discreet and crafty about getting information from Wells about the prison facility while still making it seem that her primary interest was in the doubt cast upon Mr. Folesworth's true identity. The woman was something of an artist.

Maeko sat back, holding her silence through the meeting and admiring the skill with which Em moved Wells from subject to subject and dug facts out that even he appeared surprised to discover he knew. That was, Maeko suspected, one of the critical skills that made a detective good at their job. A skill she would have to study if she wanted to work with this woman, though she still wasn't sure how involved she wanted to get in the detective business.

Wells looked like a wrung-out linen when the detective was done with him, though there was grim satisfaction in the set of his jaw and the calm in his eyes.

He appeared to be a man who had found peace with his new role. As they wrapped up, Maeko tapped her shoulder when Wells wasn't watching and Macak promptly climbed up. She watched Em leave the coach, watched the door shut. With one hand stroking Macak's head and the other held calmly in her lap, she counted to 30 then, just as Wells reached up to knock on the roof, she reached for the door.

"Hold on. I forgot to ask her something."

Wells paused, his hand stopping a mere inch from the roof. "I don't think—"

"It'll only take a second," she added as she tossed open the door and climbed out. She trotted after the detective, Macak digging in painfully to secure his position.

Em must have heard her coming. Her hand sank to her hip, brushing the long coat out of the way of her gun as she spun around to face her pursuer. Their eyes met and the detective's hand relaxed away from the gun. She gave Maeko a chastising look.

"You shouldn't run up—"

A loud crack rang through the air. Time froze for an instant in the wake of the noise. Em's eyes went wide. She staggered forward and into Maeko whose momentum made it impossible to avoid the falling woman. Macak leapt clear before they hit the ground, the weight of the other woman pressing down on her. Another crack rang out. She craned her head around in time to see the guard fall like a sack of flour from the coach seat, his gun dropping from a limp hand.

Macak crouched by her head, his fur standing up and his ears flat back.

Maeko jerked an arm free and jabbed the cat with a finger. "Get!"

The prod sent him sprinting back to the nearest hiding place, the coach, a streak of black and white that disappeared into the dark interior between the legs of the ex-Lit now peering warily out with a gun in hand.

The next shot came from a dark alley. There was a sound of shattering glass and someone fell out of a second story window to the street, someone in a Literati uniform. Maeko shook Em. The woman made a worrisome choking sound. Not dead then. Not yet. She didn't seem capable of moving herself though, so Maeko shoved her off and rose to a crouch. The next gunshot brought a cry of pain from the dark alley and a tall man in a wide-brimmed hat staggered out, falling in the street after a few struggling steps.

Rueben.

She leaned down to check Em. Blood soaked her coat, spreading from a bullet hole just inside of her left shoulder blade. Another shot rang out. Something whizzed past Maeko where her head had been seconds before. A cold sweat broke out on her neck and her mouth went dry. Em needed help, but she couldn't stay in the open like this or she'd end up no better off.

When she bolted toward the coach, two more shots rang out. One hit the side of the coach next to the open door, sending up splinters of wood around the impact site. Wells ducked back in, and Maeko skidded to a halt. She met the cowering coachman's eyes and mouthed *Go*. He didn't need to be told twice. He slapped the traces hard and the horses, already bunched and dancing with fear, were more than happy to bolt away, jerking the coach so hard that Wells fell inside and the door swung shut on his startled expression.

She twisted around. Her eyes touched on Em and on Rueben in quick succession. Both lay still. Dead, unconscious, or playing dead? She hoped for the latter.

She broke into a run, putting all her energy into getting out of there before she joined the body count. This was her city. The short time living in comfort wasn't enough to make her forget the secrets of survival on the streets. Another three shots rang out before she sprinted down a dark alley and left the open street behind. The last shots had come from two different directions. Perhaps Amos was there somewhere, fighting back. If so, she hoped he got to Em before it was too late, if that time hadn't already passed.

She ran as fast as she could, navigating dark, but familiar streets made menacing by creeping fog and fear. Cold air burned her throat raw. She kept her legs pumping, refusing to slow until she was sure no one followed. The Lits clearly weren't looking to make arrests this time. They'd gone straight to shooting without even letting anyone know they were there first. No warnings. No negotiation. Just killing.

Once she got away from the fog coming off the river, the moon was nearly full in a partly overcast sky, giving enough light to the evening streets to help her along her way while providing plenty of shadow for her to stay hidden in. She worked an indirect route toward Cheapside where the Pirate-friendly taverns should be entertaining a lively enough crowd for one small street rat to get lost in. Maybe Barman would be game for letting her hide away in his pub, though his charity might have been worn out with Heldie's murder, not that he had any way of knowing she'd been present on that unfortunate occasion.

She sprinted down another narrow street, her breath now coming in labored gasps, and burst out onto Cheapside, only to skid to an abrupt halt.

CHAPTER SIXTEEN

A tense, shifting crowd packed the street and several Literati officers had the road blocked just a few yards east of where she emerged. Angry shouts bounced back and forth between the Lits and the crowd, many of whom stood armed with guns and a diverse array of knives or makeshift clubs. Without warning, a brick hurtled across her path from somewhere in the crowd, busting noisily through the glass of the shop window next to her. Her breath caught in her throat and she ducked down in case more projectiles were on the way.

With the crash of the glass, the street went wild and the first third of the crowd charged the barricade shouting something about Pirates and freedom while more people began hurling projectiles at the shop windows. Maeko threw her hands over her head and scurried to the opposite corner to hunker down and assess the situation.

A series of rapid gunshots ripped through the air. Screams of pain and fear joined the terrifying cacophony and the front of the charge broke apart, people there falling to injuries or turning back to flee only to run into the rest of the crowd that hadn't quite caught on yet to the abrupt change of plan.

Maeko looked past the barricade to where the shots

149

had originated from and instant terror froze her in place.

Behind the barricade amidst the Literati were several rugged looking bludgers, each sporting a mechanical arm much like Chaff's and equipped with guns that could be concealed within the arms, which they were now firing on the crowd. At the front of the group, the duck shaped scar on his forehead not visible from this distance, but etched in place by her memory all the same, was Hatchet-face, the murderer who had left her with a substantial scar from the knife wound on her shoulder. The sour stench of him filled her nose though she knew there was no way she could smell him from that distance. It was a pungent recollection. As vivid as the feel of his rough hands grabbing at her and his panting breath in her face.

Her hand went to her stomach as if she could ward off the sudden sick feeling.

The slender weapon that rose out of Hatchet-face's new false arm fired faster than any of the others and had substantial recoil judging from the way his torso jerked with each shot. A feral grin curled his lips and his dead eyes shone with feverish light, getting brighter as his victims fell before the onslaught. Full panic gripped the crowd now.

Someone plowed into Maeko, driving her to the ground and falling over her in their haste to get away. The bloke flailed, kicking her several times as he scampered to his feet, not giving her so much as a glance when he pounded a boot down on her gut as he took off again. The air burst from her and she fought the need to curl around the pain, forcing herself to her hands and knees in order to scurry back down the side street. A few feet back from the corner, she pushed up against a wall to avoid further trampling by the people now fleeing down that way and pulled her knees in tight to her chest. She closed her eyes, trying to get back the air that her long run and the blow to the gut had taken from her. She couldn't run again, not quite yet, but she had to get away before the Lits found her. Before *he* found her.

A shudder passed through her.

They gave a built-in weapon to a convicted murderer? Have they gone mad?

An explosion like the one that blew her mother's house to rubble shook the air, turning the world to silence. Hot air blasted her from the street, rocking her head to the side, and the people just starting down her way were flung through the air. One landed in front of her, the back of his clothing and the flesh beneath scalded and torn. Hazel eyes stared blankly at her from his youthful dirt smudged face and a pocket watch lay on the ground, its chain wound in his still fingers.

Just a street rat taking advantage of a distracted crowd. She would likely have done the same only a short time ago.

I could have been you.

Her stomach threatened to revolt and she swallowed hard. Another explosion split the air, this one going off further down, in the direction of the Literati barricade. The Pirates fighting back perhaps?

Time to go.

She pushed to her feet and ran back the way she had come, turning off down a familiar street that would take her to the big Cheapside lurk where she'd stayed with

Chaff. By now, if anyone other than Em had followed her there when she fled after Lucian's death, they would have searched the place and lost interest in it again. It should be a safe enough place to hole up and try to come up with a new plan now that her idea to run off and work with Em had been violently altered.

#

Maeko walked through the burned out husk of the old lurk, scratching at dried blood on her right arm. Something had cut a shallow gash there. Shrapnel from the explosion perhaps. It stung now. A distant pain that couldn't quite cut through the numbness that dulled her thoughts. She wouldn't have believed the hollow inside could grow any vaster, but this proved that it could. One of the places she'd made a home of sorts growing up now lay in ruins beneath her feet. One more place she could never go back to.

With each slow step through the charred pile of timber and stone, she could see the building as it had been, a broken down, scarred old husk of a building teeming with hidden life. Kids of all ages sought sanctuary within those walls, sharing the tales of their latest exploits in the only place they felt like they belonged. Memory recreated each room in sharp relief, moments from her past jumping up to rebuild countless hours of her life spent within those walls. Many of those moments came accompanied by Chaff's bright blue eyes and easy mischievous grin.

She stopped walking and gazed around. This was the spot. This was where the room Chaff made his own had been, where he had nursed her back to health after saving her from the big dog-torturing bludger who'd tried to kill her. She remembered his kiss as a soft warmth on her now cold and dry lips. She pressed her cheek into her hand, recalling the feel of his strong bare chest against her face.

She closed her eyes and Ash's pale green eyes rose up in her mind. She chewed at her lower lip.

I'm sorry Ash. I didn't know I loved him. Not that it matters now.

Now she had no one. Not Ash. Not Chaff. Not Em. Not even the one companion she'd hoped to keep with her through all of this.

Macak.

She sank to her knees, bits of debris biting into them as her scant weight rested down. There wasn't much hope. Without Em to convince them, the Bobbies wouldn't intervene and with the weapons the Lits already had operational, there was no way an attack on the prison would be anything less than disastrous for both sides.

The bright night had turned overcast and rain began to fall. Fat, grimy drops of wet pattered around her. She watched the way it made the black of charred wood turn blacker in the dim light. The fat drops slid through her hair, one running cold down the back of her neck and eliciting a small shiver.

Footsteps crunched through the debris behind her. Her heartbeat barely quickened, too weighted down with defeat to care of what danger the sound might foretell. Besides, if the person wanted to shoot her, they would have done so already. If they wanted to capture her, they wouldn't approach with a weary trudge that timed well to the slow thud of her beaten down heart.

A shadow fell over her, a darker patch in the night. After a moment, she noticed that the rain stopped hitting her head. An umbrella? Out of the corner of her eye, she saw the toes of heavy black boots peeking out from under creased brown slacks that were rolled up twice.

Amos?

"How'd you find me?"

The booted feet shifted on the rubble with soft crunching sounds. When she glanced up at his face, Amos was staring into the night, not at anything in particular that she could see. The pain of the debris poking into her knees was beginning to break through the daze. She stared at the ground again and let it hurt.

"Em told me to find you," he muttered, just barely loud enough for her to make out his words. "This was one of the first places she thought you might come."

"She's a good detective."

"Was."

The hollow in her chest grew, expanding to the point that her ribs and throat and gut all ached with it. She would explode with the pressure of that growing despair, that miserable nothing that bellowed within her.

Em is dead. "Em is dead?"

Amos made a small affirmative sound that twisted in her gut and at the base of her skull like a needle pushing into the nerves there.

This was all the provocation Drake needed. He would charge the moment his battleship was ready and blast his vengeance upon the Literati and Thaddeus. They deserved it. Some of them did. Not all though. How many were like Captain Garrett, forced to work for the enemy. How many were as Wells had been, blindly hoping that they'd chosen the right side. Unwilling to see the foul deeds being done because they so desperately needed to be one of the good guys. How many were like her, merely committing their crimes because they needed to get by, blaming society for making it necessary.

She swallowed around the knife blade lodged in her throat. "Rueben?"

His silence was the only answer she needed.

"Did the coach get away?"

"I don't know."

Macak.

"This little guy did though." He opened his jacket and pulled a familiar black and white feline out, placing him on the ground. "Jumped out the coach window when he realized you weren't going with him."

She picked Macak up and held him tight, her tears sliding warm down her cheeks and into his fur. She swallowed again. It didn't help the pain. "What now?"

"It's over."

Was it? Was that it? Were they helpless now? Stuck sitting back and watching as things played out? Was there nothing they could do?

She chewed at her lip for a few seconds, feeling Macak's heartbeat fast and strong under one hand, then looked up at the stocky man.

"Amos, why can't you go to the Bobbies? I can tell you everything that Wells told Em."

He looked down at her now, measuring her with his gaze. "I suppose I could try it. Better yet, why don't you just come with me? You can tell them yourself."

She got to her feet slowly, wincing at the complaining of her knees as they moved off the unforgiving surface. Turning around, she stared out into the dark back the way she'd come.

"I can't. I have someone else I have to pay a visit."

Amos peered at her through shrewd narrowed eyes. "You've got a plan?"

"I'm getting one. It's not much, but it's better than giving up."

"Care to fill me in?"

She shook her head slowly. "You worry about the Bobbies. That's enough of a job for one person."

"Dangerous, eh?"

Possibly fatal. She shrugged noncommittally.

He turned to face the same direction and peered into the darkness with her. "Guess you'd best tell me what I need to know then. I'm not about to let you down too."

She doubted he'd let Em down, but now wasn't the time to argue about it. Instead, she called up the conversation Em and Wells had in the coach and began to recount it for Amos in as much detail as she could.

CHAPTER SEVENTEEN

The other survivors of the attack arrived as they were speaking. Wells knew enough, somehow, to direct the coach driver to the destroyed lurk. She didn't ask how he knew. Though she was beginning to suspect he'd been an ally to the kids of the street before he chose to join the Pirates. His arrival was a somber one. The remaining Lits were killed, giving Wells and the coachman enough time to gather Em, Rueben, and the guard before more arrived on the scene. That meant they had to share the coach with their lost comrades if they were going to get back to the manor, and she needed to get back to the manor.

She needed help.

She needed Drake's help most of all.

Amos shook her hand, somber and professional, gave Macak a scratch between the ears, then headed out to catch a hansom to start his task of continuing Em's work with the Bobbies. With a gut full of dread, Makeo climbed into the coach with Wells and they did their best to find seating amidst the three bodies.

Tears ran quiet down her cheeks. She tried not to look at the dead, Em especially where they had propped her up against the far side, slumped into the corner as though passed out drunk. As prickly as the detective could be, she'd still been a mentor of sorts and a chance for a different future. The pain was fresh and raw. The stench of blood flipped her stomach and made her head ache. She had thought about riding up with the driver, but both she and Wells were too easily recognized by the people who wanted them dead and Macak was safer inside.

"You've got a plan hatching," Wells observed in a low voice, almost as if afraid to disturb their resting companions.

It was funny in a horrible kind of way. It made her want to both weep and laugh.

"I don't know. I need to talk to Drake and…" she gave him a level look, "…and I think I need you to be there when I do."

Wells glanced at the bodies and something flashed in his eyes. Something cold and hard with a lethal edge. Good. He looked at her then, that hard edge remaining, and gave a single solemn nod.

They didn't speak again. The ride out of town was tense, both of them all too aware that any passing Lit might noticed the damage to the coach from the flying bullets. At one point the driver turned the horses suddenly and sped them up, perhaps to avoid such an encounter. Rueben, who was propped on her side, started to fall toward her and Wells jumped up, stepping over the legs of the guard on the floor to catch him with an almost frantic manner, as though her life depended on it. Even though she knew the dead man couldn't bring her any harm, she appreciated the effort more than she could manage to say around the lump in her throat. When he sat back down, she tried to convey her gratitude in her expression. He averted his gaze.

They didn't make it far into the manor grounds before someone noticed the damage and alarms sounded, bringing people rushing out to meet the coach. Maeko had the door open before they stopped fully, hopping out with Macak in arms. Wells almost stepped on her heels as they both hurried to get away from the death within.

They had barely gotten free of the coach before Drake manifested seemingly out of nowhere to beat everyone else to them. He took a quick glance inside the coach, a grim expression bringing that predatory look down over his features, making him someone to be wary of again. He pinned the two of them with the barbed arrows of his gaze.

"We…"

"…need to talk," Maeko finished for him and turned to start walking toward the manor.

Wells joined her without question or hesitation.

Drake paused long enough to toss out some directions for the temporary management of the dead, then trotted after them and fell into stride next to her. Macak gave him a quick look and meowed a few criticisms of his own, earning a thoughtful look from the man. When a cat felt you needed a talking to, it was time to consider what you might need to work on in your life.

Several people started to approach, their worried looks asking what had happened, but the stern expressions on the group as they made their way purposefully to Drakes office were enough to dissuade everyone except Crimson, who wasn't dissuaded by much of anything from what Maeko had observed. Drake gave her a slight nod of acknowledgement, making no effort to discourage her joining and Maeko nodded to herself. It was as it should be. The two needed to be partners in this. She had no doubt that Crimson was good for Drake and, somehow, he was good for her too.

Once inside the office, Drake stepped behind his desk, Crimson choosing a spot to the side of it, her position putting her a few inches closer on his side, but also neutral enough to be supportive of theirs.

"What happened?"

"We were attacked by Lits. They took out Em, Reuben and your man," Wells explained. "There weren't a lot of them. Few enough that we were able to take them down once we knew they were there and collect our dead, but they've gotten a lot bolder."

Drake started to curse under his breath.

Macak extracted himself from her arms and curled around her shoulders, lending his warmth to bolster her confidence.

"That isn't the important part," Maeko said.

Drake gave her an icy glare. "Three of our people are dead. That seems rather weighty to me."

She drew in a deep breath and exhaled. "It is, but there's more. They're putting criminals, murderers even, out on the street with dangerous weapons. I recognized some I saw from the designs in Lucian's study. They're bent on killing more than just a few Pirates."

"Us," Drake countered, dropping the weighted word between them.

She looked at him for a long moment then lifted

Macak with a shrug that somehow compelled the cat to press his head into her cheek and purr more loudly. "Us. I think they mean to exterminate us completely. Em suspected them of planning something bigger."

"A change of government?"

"Perhaps."

He was looking at her thoughtfully now. "What do we do about it?"

Now she stared at him for a *very* long moment. Soon she realized that Wells was also watching her. Expecting. Were they really asking her? How had this happened? The street rat was being asked for her advice on how to proceed in a battle that would end in death for some.

"I need to get back inside the prison."

Drake's features turned to stone. "You are not taking my airship in there again."

"No, I'm not," she agreed, creating a fracture in his hard scowl. "Is the battleship ready?"

"Very close." Drake answered with a slow nod.

"Good. I need at least 12 hours at the prison. Then you can attack the facility."

Crimson was looking more and more unhappy, but Drake was starting to look interested. Wells simply looked as though he wasn't quite sure how to look, his gaze bouncing back and forth between the two Pirates.

"How do you plan to get inside?"

"I'm going to go to the Airship tower. I think I can convince the thugs Thaddeus has watching that place to take me to him at the prison if I tell them you abandoned me after Em was shot and that I'm willing to tell them how to find you now."

Wells and Crimson were shaking their heads. At least Wells had chosen a side now, even if it was the wrong one.

"Kitten, those men will kill you before you have a chance to make the offer," Crimson objected.

Maeko kept her gaze locked with Drake's. "No, they won't. Thaddeus is greedy and obsessed. He wants to know where the Pirates are. He wants to destroy every trace of them... us. He said he would let his thugs kill me, but now that he knows I'm in deep with the Pirates I don't believe he'll let them do so without trying one more time to get what he wants out of me."

Well's spoke up this time. "Are you willing to bet your life on that?"

Again, she kept her eyes on Drake, but she scratched Macak's head to quiet the terrified tremble inside and nodded.

"What if Thaddeus isn't at the prison?"

Something she had considered. "I'll tell him Ash deserted with me and that I need to speak to Captain Garrett and see for myself that he's all right before I'll give them any information."

Drake was quiet.

"What if they decide to torture you for the information?"

Crimson's question fed the tremble and it was all she could do to keep her voice from shaking when she spoke.

"We have to stop their production at that prison or the Pirates will be destroyed and a lot of innocent people are going to get hurt in the process. I came upon a standoff between the Lits new forces and some Pirates in Cheapside. They don't care who gets hurt in the crossfire. We're running out of time. I have to try. Give me 12 hours to find a way to get Captain Garrett to safety. If I haven't succeeded by then..." Now her voice did shake a little. "... then I was wrong about Thaddeus."

Drake met her gaze for a minute or more, unmoving, unspeaking, but saying so much. An understanding passed between them and she learned something about both of them in that moment. They were similar creatures, she realized. They were both determined to try and protect the ones they cared about to the point that they had trouble letting anyone care for them. They both knew they would put themselves at risk and that letting the ones they were trying to protect care for them in turn was likely to bring those individuals pain in the long run. It was the reason he wanted to tell her no. It was also the reason he would let her go.

"I'll need a coach to take me back into the city. Preferably not the one I arrived in. I don't think I can..."

Drake nodded, not requiring her to finish.

"No." Crimson and Wells spoke in unison.

Crimson walked over to Drake, a hint of desperation in her imploring gaze. "You can't let this happen. Thaddeus will kill her."

"Maybe I should go with you," Wells suggested in a low tone, trying not to interrupt the hushed exchange now happening between Drake and Crimson.

Maeko gave him a hard look and he flushed.

"You're right. That idea was bollocks." He shoved his hands in his pockets, becoming an awkward boy for a moment.

Maeko smiled at him, ignoring Drake and Crimson's hushed, but heated words. The argument was irrelevant anyway. She was going.

"I appreciate the offer."

He simply shrugged, his cheeks flushing a hint brighter.

Maeko turned back to Drake and he held a hand up to silence Crimson, the gesture firm though there was softness in his eyes for her. "Have you considered asking Ash or Chaff to go with you?"

She thought she was beyond feeling any more pain from loss, but that one sentence twisted the dagger in her gut twice. Em had been the future that was going to help her move on without them.

Without them.

Regardless, of where those relationships stood, Chaff and Ash were still alive, still relatively safe. She'd had to watch Em dying, she didn't want to do the same with either of them. She had come more than close enough with Chaff all too recently. This time no one else was going to be at risk.

She shook her head.

"The battleship isn't quite ready. Give me a day to pull a few things together. You can eat and rest. You'll need to be at the top of your game if you're going to walk into their hands and have any hope of walking out again, let alone any chance of rescuing Garrett."

Stubborn resistance swelled within her. If she waited here, she would have too much time on her hands. Time in which she might find herself dwelling on things, or worse, talking to people. There were people here she couldn't bear to face. Words rose into her mouth and stormed over her tongue, marching for her lips. Bold words. Words of defiance.

Macak rubbed his head against her cheek again, his purr a kiss of calm and reason. She deflated.

Words born of fear and foolishness tumbled back down her throat.

"One day," she managed, then turned and walked from the room.

I t turned out that, after a good meal, getting some rest wasn't such a challenge after all. Maeko crawled into the comfy bed in the room she shared with her mother and cried into her pillow, mourning a woman she had admired. Cared for in some way, despite her caustic temperament. A woman who had offered the chance of a future as something more than a dollymop. A woman who had accomplished remarkable things and deserved to be missed by someone.

Macak curled up against her and began to purr until he soothed her to sleep with his warmth, a few tears still dripping to the pillow as she dozed off. She slept hard on through the rest of the day and most of the night, partly waking a few times during the day when Tomoe or Crimson came to let Macak out for a bathroom break, but somehow never when they brought him back. He would simply be curled against her again when next she stirred.

When she finally fully woke before dawn the next morning, she could only assume Tomoe had slept in another room to avoid disturbing her, for she still shared the bed only with the warm cat who began purring the moment she opened her eyes, his big yellow eyes blinking as though he too had woken from a deep

166

slumber.

She felt rested. Not any less sorrowful or determined, but rested at least and less likely to make foolish mistakes for it. Not that walking into the hands of her enemies didn't have many of the makings of a very foolish choice, but she had to try something. She had to give Ash a chance to have a happy family again and she was willing to risk everything she had to do it, including her life. Besides, she had a better chance of getting close to Garrett than anyone else did.

As absurd as it was, she believed Thaddeus would talk to her. There was something between them. Some unintentional connection that drew him to her. He may have killed his own brother, but the tears he had wept on top of the airship tower had been real. She was a connection to the blood kin he had sacrificed to his ambition. A connection that he resented, but only because he felt some guilt over what he had done and that guilt made him hesitate when it came to eliminating her. There was also an unexpected respect in his regard when last they crossed paths, perhaps for her tenacity. If Bennett didn't kill her on sight, then she could probably talk Thaddeus into at least letting her speak to Garrett. Getting Garrett out of the prison was going to be a different level of challenge altogether, but one she was willing to face.

She forced herself to leave the warm bed and wash up at the basin. Then she waited until Macak took his place on her shoulders before heading out into the gloom of the predawn manor. Below, where the battleship and other projects were being finished in preparation for an assault on the prison, there would be an unending bustle of activity, but up here it was mostly servants moving about on their everyday tasks.

She made her way out to the back gardens where Macak could find a private spot to do his business. As the cat began prowling about in search of the proper spot, occasionally distracted from his task by the odd insect or rustling leaf that needed slaying, she found a quiet spot on a stone bench. A mist obscured the vast lands around the manor, making it feel as though the house itself and this garden were an island unto themselves in a vast sea of nothing. She closed her eyes, breathing in the moist, chilly air to clear her head.

Her eyes snapped open when she heard footsteps crunching on the gravel walk and she glanced about for a place to hide, but it was already too late. Ash and Chaff were halfway between her bench and the back door and were very obviously coming her way.

Wait. Ash AND Chaff? Together?

There was something about them walking along side-by-side that made her uneasy after all that had happened. It would be bad enough to have to face one of them right now, but both at the same time? That was just cruel. For a few seconds, she considered wandering off as though she hadn't noticed them. The odds of her making a successful escape, if she was indeed their goal, were slim though. Neither boy was the type to let her brush them off that easily.

Sensing her sudden anxiety, Macak leapt up on the bench and plopped himself down on her lap. She couldn't bring herself to toss him off, which meant she was stuck. She gave the cat a suspicious look. Perhaps he hadn't jumped up there for her benefit after all.

The two boys stopped a few feet in front of her, regarding her with a matching solemnity.

"Mae," Ash started. He faltered then, meeting her eyes for a second, before his gaze slid away.

"Maeko," Chaff stepped in, his tone somehow both formal and timid, neither of which suited him. "We came out here to apologize."

"Yes," Ash confirmed. "We both owe you apologies."

Hope and a wealth of sorrow tightened around her middle like a corset being cinched. She said nothing. Speaking might break the moment, or wake her from this odd, awkward dream. She stroked Macak's head and kept her own council for the moment. The mist drifted in between them and the manor, isolating the four of them in their own tiny sliver of the world.

Ash swallowed hard. "I know you would have saved my dad that night at the prison if there were any way to do it. I was angry at myself more than at you because I felt like I failed, but I took it out on you. I treated you terribly when all you ever did was try to help me and I'm sorry."

"And I know you never meant for me to get hurt," Chaff began, stepping in before the silence could stretch. "You never mean for anyone to get hurt. You only did what you did because you care too much sometimes, because you don't want *anyone* to get hurt, and that's something I love about you. I wouldn't have you any other way. Besides," a dagger twisted in her chest when he glanced down at his mechanical hand and a wry smirk touched his lips, "Drake did give this arm a few nice additions the old one lacked."

"He sure did." Ash added with a tentative, boyish smile. "It's the dog's bollocks."

Chaff tossed Ash a quick scoundrel grin and Maeko discreetly pinched herself to see if she could maybe wake up before this got any stranger.

"The point is," Chaff continued, serious again, "we both care a lot about you. We know you're planning to try and help Ash's father again before Drake moves on the prison and we want to help you."

"But Drake needs me to finish up some things for the battleship if it's going to be ready fast enough to…" Ash trailed off, looking a bit crestfallen, and nodded to Chaff.

"What we decided was that perhaps I should go with you. I'm not doing anything here except taking up space."

Maeko was nearly overwhelmed with the urge to hug or hit each of them. She lifted Macak into her arms as she stood to make both options impossible. She gave them a suspicious scowl.

"Did Crimson put you two up to this?"

Both boys looked mildly insulted, though there was a hint of flush in Ash's cheeks that told her she hadn't missed the mark by much. He didn't have Chaff's skill in the fine arts of deception.

Chaff kicked the dirt with one shoe, knowing full well that she, of all people, would know when he was dodging the truth. "No."

"But?"

"Drake might have said something," Ash admitted.

Drake?

That surprised her a bit. The wealthy Pirate was an

odd one.

"I don't suppose it matters. I think you're both barmy, but I do appreciate the apologies. I'm sorry too, for everything that's gone wrong, but I believe we might be able to make some of those things right." She gave Chaff a speculative look. "Are you healed enough to be out running around?"

He nodded, a flicker of some deep sorrow and shame shadowing his features for a moment. Given their last encounter, she suspected she knew where the shame came from. "I'm well enough. There's still healing to be done, but the arm is functional and the pain isn't so bad."

She had a feeling he was understating a fair bit, but the cogs were already spinning and the task she had for him wasn't going to require much physical exertion.

"Good enough." She looked him up and down once more and wrinkled her nose. "We need to find you some better clothes. Someone around here's got to have some decent togs they'd be willing to loan you. C'mon."

She started toward the house. It was only a few seconds before the boys fell into step with her and she felt, for an odd moment, rather like Em must have felt with Amos and Rueben always on her heels.

The thought of Em brought the woman's last moment back to her mind in vivid detail. That expression of shock, of surprise. Death had finally caught up with her and hadn't bothered to stop and introduce himself before taking what was his to take. She remembered as vividly the hollowness in Amos's eyes. Em was gone. Rueben was gone. His world had been flipped upside down in seconds.

This had to end.

Whether the Pirates were going to make anything better or not, the Lits and their supporters had killed people and were building weapons with which they could continue to do so in greater numbers. Drake's battleship was a weapon as well, but his proclaimed intention was to use it to strike a blow to the Lits that would end their rise to power and stop the killing in the streets. The Pirates wanted to put an end to starvation and mistreatment in Literati workhouses. They wanted to lessen the gap between the rich and poor, especially when it came to access to healthier living conditions and medical care. That's what she overheard in the halls of Drake's manor. She had to hope it was true.

She swallowed a lump in her throat and held Macak a little tighter as she headed into the manor. Without too much trouble, they tracked down Crimson. It was so easy, in fact, that Maeko suspected the woman had been spying on them.

"We need to find some more..." She paused, looking Chaff up and down. The clothes they'd given him to replace the bedraggled and stained ones he'd arrived in weren't a large improvement over his typical street wear. She needed him to look upstanding and she needed to hide his arm and hand. "Some more distinguished togs that fit well enough to pass him off as someone in service to a wealthy gent. Perhaps some gentleman's gloves as well."

Crimson swept him once over with her discerning emerald gaze and Maeko didn't doubt that she'd estimated his measurements in that quick once over with admirable accuracy.

"I think we can manage that without too much difficulty. Anything is going to be a touch loose. You're still a bit undernourished from your stay with the Lits, but I don't doubt we can make you look upstanding enough." Crimson squinted her eyes at his head, looking dubious. "Especially if you let Tomoe give you a quick trim."

Maeko met Chaff's eyes. His brows raised as if to ask if that was necessary or perhaps simply checking to see if she were on board with the idea. Either way, she trusted Crimson's opinion so she gave him a nod.

"While you two are working on that, I need to talk to Drake."

"He's down in the underground workshop," Ash offered. "I can take you down there."

This time, Maeko glanced at Chaff, seeking his approval. It wasn't as though she wouldn't go should he disapprove and she suspected he knew that, but perhaps showing that she at least cared what he thought would help smooth their relationship a bit. The lack of hesitation before his nod made her wonder what had passed between the two boys in her absence. She did notice that Ash looked a touch put out by her seeking Chaff's approval, so all was not sweetness and light between the three of them. At least a peace treaty of some kind had apparently been negotiated.

She met Ash's eyes, wishing the flicker of sorrow that lingered there was something she could fix, but, for all that she cared for him, she didn't love him that way and anything she did to try to fix this would only prolong the process of healing. It was time to move on.

"Let's go."

CHAPTER NINETEEN

Maeko and Ash left Chaff in Crimson's capable hands and started off in the direction of the underground hangar and workshop. Macak draped himself comfortably around her neck, a superheated, if slightly weighty, scarf.

"Can I ask what happened in the last day? I didn't think either of you wanted anything to do with me." *Let alone with each other.*

Ash shrugged. "I can't speak for Chaff, but I got a solid tongue-lashing from Drake for the way I was treating you. I was devastated when you came out of that prison with Chaff and not with my dad. It was like that night at the orphanage all over again, when you weren't able to get to Sam before Em did. I hated myself for not being there to protect my brother in the first place back then and I hated myself for not being there for my dad when they took him. I also resented you for getting what you wanted. You had Chaff back and I had nothing then, not even you. It wasn't your fault, I know, but I couldn't help imagining that you had just given up on saving my dad once you knew Chaff was safe."

"I wouldn't do that to you or him. I hope you know that."

174

He gave her a sideways glance and a tentative, self-conscious smile tugged at his lips. "I realize that, but I was also burning half-mad with jealousy. It's no reason to treat you the way I have been, but a terrible part of me had hoped that you wouldn't be able to save him."

Maeko took a deep breath to silence a spark of anger and scratched Macak's head. "I'm pretty sure I knew that too."

"Can you forgive me?"

She glanced at him. His furrowed brow and the worried lines around his eyes said he thought she might not.

"I suppose so." She sidestepped, bumping into him playfully with her shoulder.

A relieved smile banished the worry and he bumped her back, almost knocking her off her feet. He was a solid block of muscle, especially after spending so much time down working on the airship of late. Quite the opposite of Chaff's lean, lanky form, grown thinner with his recent ordeal. So, different, the two of them, and yet both so dear.

"I know you're going in there to try and save my dad again and I know better than to argue with you about it. All I can ask is that you try not to get hurt. For my sake and your mother's and, yeah, even for Chaff's sake."

"I'm not going to pretend it isn't dangerous, but I'll try to come out in one piece."

They stopped at the bottom of the dark stairwell before the door into the underground lab and hangar when she realized they didn't have a code for the lock... or did they?

Ash walked up to the door and turned the dial to a chorus of clicks and mechanical grumblings until it shifted open. She felt a small pang of jealousy that he had been entrusted with the keys to the secret lair, so to speak, and she had not, but he was helping build the battleship, so it did make sense.

As soon as she stepped inside, the battleship commanded her attention. It was big. Sleek. Black. Somehow beautiful. It had been finished to look like Drake's stealthy matte black personal airship, but it was so much larger, filling the massive space of the underground hangar. Lightweight cannons attached to the four corners of the two long gondolas stripped the airborne whale of a ship of any semblance of innocence. A lethal leviathan.

"What do you think of her?"

Maeko wasn't sure if she'd walked up beside Drake or he up beside her. She found herself smiling and felt immediately guilty for it. This was a machine of death. Or perhaps it should be looked at as a machine of intimidation, intended to bring peace and a better life… at a dire cost to those who stood in the way of such things.

"She's magnificent." She turned to Drake, catching the smile of a proud father pulling at the corners of his mouth. "Is she ready?"

"Your boy here is going to help me finish fine tuning some things with the cannons," he answered with a nod to Ash. "She's ready to fly now."

"Good. I'm ready to head into town. Chaff is going with me. He's going to help me suss out the situation at the Tower. Once I'm on my way to the prison, he'll head back here and let you know so you can get the timing right."

Drake nodded. "I'd hoped you would work something like that out once these two dunces got over themselves and realized how unfairly they were treating you."

Ash flushed, tucking his hands in his pockets and staring at the floor. He must have gotten quite the earful from Drake.

"I need to ask you a favor."

A crackle of dread danced over her nerves, but she owed him a great deal. For taking her and her mother in. For bringing the boys around. "I'll help if I can."

"That's all I can ask." His gaze moved to the area opposite the airship where various inventions were being worked on by a small handful of individuals with monocles, myriad complex tools, and identical engrossed expressions. "If you're able, when you find Garrett, see if you can get the blueprints for the work they're doing at that facility."

"They're making weapons," she objected, putting her foot down in her mind. She would not aid in the further spread of devices of death.

"Mostly, but Lucian was never really a maker of war. There may be some technology in those blueprints that has other useful applications. I see no reason to let the creations of a brilliant man go to ruin."

Maeko stroked Macak's side, the tips of her fingers brushing against his clockwork leg. What had Thaddeus said? *Cats with missing legs aren't that easy to come by, but they're easy enough to make.* That didn't mean that Lucian was all bad, but it certainly lost him a substantial chunk of respect in her regard. Still, Drake's point wasn't wrong.

"I'll do my best."

Drake gave a nod. "Again, that is all I can ask. It's far more important that you and Garrett come out alive. If we lose that knowledge, we will regain it another way. If you get lucky, then we'll celebrate a bit of good fortune later, agreed?"

"Agreed."

The big door behind them opened and Wells entered carrying a folded paper. Maeko was surprised to realize that Drake must have given the ex-Lit the code as well. With a single elegant gesture, Drake directed them all to a nearby table where Wells quickly began unfolding the paper.

"I asked Wells if he could remember enough of the prison layout to give you some extra guidance," Drake explained as the map Wells had given her of the prison when she visited him at JAHF for help rescuing Chaff was spread out before them. She had thought she left it in her room. Perhaps Tomoe had found it for them.

Many new details had been hand drawn in with various helpful tips and labels added. Wells quickly set to work pointing out where the guards tended to spend the most time, where Garrett and the blueprints were being kept when he was there, and where the least protected entrances had been. He and Maeko went over it all several times while Ash and Drake looked on in silence. When she felt like she had it committed to memory she nodded to Wells.

"Thank you. This is invaluable."

Wells shrugged. "I wanted to help. After all, you

worked your way under my skin like you seem to do with most people."

Drake chuckled and Ash heaved a sigh.

Maeko felt her cheeks reddening. Unsure what to say to that, she muttered another thank you and turned to Drake. "I'm ready."

"Are you going to take the map?" Wells asked.

She looked it over one more time. "I can't. If they find it on me it will expose my lies and I'll be killed for certain."

Wells paled and began to fold the map up again.

Drake nodded. "The coach should be waiting."

#

A short time later, she gave Ash a long hug outside a coach in front of the manor. Too long perhaps to pretend that she didn't suspect she might not make it back, but she wanted to let him know he was important to her and she was afraid to say too much lest her voice betray her fear. Drake stood watching them from a second-floor balcony, his face shadowed so she couldn't see his expression, but Tomoe and Crimson were standing up there with him. She almost felt sorry for him. Neither woman looked pleased with the turn of events, Tomoe especially. Maeko gave her mother a small wave over Ash's shoulder. Tomoe lifted her hand in response, looking like she might burst in to tears.

Maeko looked away and stepped back from the hug, not sure what to say.

Macak sprinted past and leapt up into the coach when Chaff walked outside to join them. Chaff was dressed in fancy businessmen's attire, his hair neatly combed and perhaps a smidge shorter. The hand of his mechanical arm was hidden beneath dapper gloves. He almost would have looked like his normal old self if seeing him dressed that well didn't strike her so odd. He looked distinguished. He looked handsome, though she still rather preferred him in his usual scoundrel street clothes.

She realized she'd been staring a little too long when he gave her a teasing smirk and she flushed, glancing away.

There was a hint of envy behind Ash's good-natured smile, but he made no comment.

"See you soon, mate," Chaff offered as he walked past them and stepped into the coach.

"You better," Ash answered.

Still tongue-tied, Maeko started to turn away.

"Gunb... ganbun..." Ash flushed and she couldn't stop a soft giggle. He chuckled in response and gave up. "Good luck."

"Ganbatte," she answered and stepped into the coach after Chaff.

There was a moment of awkwardness when she entered the dim interior. Chaff had settled on the far end of one seat, leaving several options open. Should she sit beside him? Were the emotional wounds between them sufficiently healed? Or should she sit across from him? If she sat across from him, would that send the wrong message?

Macak, the glorious cat, leapt up and stretched out long next to Chaff on the bench and Maeko, that option removed, went to sit across from him. Chaff scratched the cat's head with his right hand, his movement a little awkward as though trying to weigh the oddness of using his non-dominant hand against the strangeness of the artificial limb.

"He's a smart little beast, isn't he?"

She smiled, feeling an odd shyness as she did so. Had he felt the same awkwardness she did? "He certainly is."

Once the door was shut, the coach began to move. Without any holes in her clothing to pick at, Maeko forced her hands to settle in her lap and stared at them.

"I know I said sorry once already, but I want you to know that I really am so sorry for how I treated you, Mae. I never really blamed you for what happened to my hand. You made your choices, but I made some choices too and one of those choices was to watch over you and try to keep you safe while you were trying to protect the people you love. I followed you knowing the risks."

Her throat twisted and tears sprung to her eyes without warning, running fast down her cheeks. She brought a hand up, meaning to brush them away, but Chaff caught her wrist in his metal hand. The grip was strong and painfully tight, though warmed a touch by the glove. She winced, and his hand loosened. His features twisted in a grimace.

"Bollocks. I'm still getting the hang of it."

A few more tears crept down her cheeks.

"It's all right." She glanced toward the hand. "Can I see it?"

His expression tightened, but he tugged the glove off and tossed it down on his thigh, holding the mechanical hand out to her. She cupped her hands under his, turning it slightly. The metal had a soft gleam in the low lighting. When he moved his fingers, myriad tiny parts moved together in silent, graceful harmony to make the motion possible.

She smiled. "It's a bit beautiful in a way."

He grimaced again. "I'm not so enamored. I can see that you're holding it, but I can't feel the softness of your skin. That's a hard thing to give up."

She scooted to the edge of her seat.

"Maybe you can't feel me here," she said, squeezing the hand. Then she touched a hand to his chest, letting it come to rest over his heart. "But can you feel me here?"

"I can," he breathed.

Macak hoped over to her side now as Chaff slid to the edge of the bench, leaning toward her in turn. "I love you, Maeko."

Her heart skipped and she moved across the remaining space between them, wrapping her arms around his neck and planting her lips on his in a rather graceless motion that pushed him back against the seat, but somehow it didn't matter. They tasted of one another like two people drinking water after hours working in the blazing sun. A few moments later she shifted around into the seat next to him, one hand still on his shoulder as though afraid he might disappear if she let go and more of those blasted tears streamed down her cheeks.

Chaff pulled off the glove on his right hand and wiped gently at a tear. Then she kissed him again, or he kissed her, she wasn't sure which. She only knew it didn't matter because, for this moment, they were exactly where they needed to be, wrapped up in each other… with Macak safely curled on the other bench pretending not to notice.

I'm going in," Chaff announced, and stood up to leave their quiet corner of the café.

Maeko put a hand over his on the table to stop him, noting that she automatically went for the flesh hand, not out of the realization that he might not respond if she'd done the other, but more from a lingering sense of guilt.

"Remember, get in and back out. Don't get into a chinwag. You only need the attendant to tell you if he's in the flat right now or expected back soon. You're representing a client who was expecting to meet with him this evening but is running a behind schedule and you want to make sure he is going to be there when your client arrives."

"I've got this, May." Chaff grinned his carefree scoundrel grin at her, his dapper grooming and distinguished togs somehow making him look both cuter and more cunning. The shirt was too loose, but careful tucking behind the vest and coat hid that.

He danced away from her playful swat with a wicked sparkle in his eyes, very much acting like his old self with his mechanical arm hidden from sight beneath jacket and glove. At the café door, he paused and gave her a wink, then straightened his collar and cuffs, the motion a little awkward as he struggled with learning complete control of the new appendage, and started across the busy street.

It was all she could do not to revert to the old habit of chewing her nails while she waited for him to return. She tried instead to focus on petting the warm ball of cat curled on the lap of her skirts under which she wore more practical trousers. It was maddening not to be in the midst of the action where she would know what was happening firsthand, but she couldn't afford to be spotted near the Airship Tower. Not yet. She had to trust Chaff to do this alone.

What if Thaddeus were there now and the guards insisted on escorting Chaff up? Or might they make him wait while they called Thaddeus or one of his thugs down to verify the disguised street rat's claims?

Chaff was clever though. His wily ways had kept him alive on the streets since he was a young boy. He wasn't about to let them get the better of him that easily and Thaddeus wasn't going to want his thugs killing random visitors in public. She had to settle down and wait. Besides, she'd never gotten this worked up over him going off to do a caper on his own before. Why the dread now? Was it because so much hinged on getting this right? Or might it have more to do with recent changes in their relationship?

Bollocks! Things had been a fair sum simpler not so long ago. Although, the changes weren't all bad. Some of their previous kisses slipped into her thoughts, and her cheeks warmed.

It felt like he was gone an hour, though the clock on the café wall said it had only been seventeen minutes… not that she was counting. The instant she saw him

strolling back across the street, it was all she could do
not to leap up and rush out to him. He wove through
coaches and foot traffic with snakelike fluidity, head
high as if he had every right to be there in his waistcoat
and gentleman's gloves. He looked more than ever like
the Chaff she'd always known. Somehow always
belonging anywhere no matter how out of place he was.
Strong, wily, and dashing. She smiled to herself and
scratched Macak under the chin.

He didn't come back into the café. Instead, he
turned and sauntered down the pavement, making sure
she had ample opportunity to spot him, and continued
toward their prearranged rendezvous spot in front of a
hatter's shop on the corner of the next block, out of
sight of the front of the Tower. She tucked a somewhat
reluctant Macak into the satchel she'd brought and
waited with forced patience until another group got up
and started toward the door. She followed close behind
and slipped out the door with them, using them as a
visual shield between her and the Tower. They turned
the wrong direction, so she went along with them,
keeping close enough to appear to be part of their group
to the casual onlooker. At the next corner, she peeled
off and went around the block, working her way back to
where Chaff would be waiting.

When she got close to the hatter's, she spotted him
standing beside a young couple that appeared to be
asking him directions. His eyes met hers for a second, a
flicker of welcome in them before he stepped in close to
the man's shoulder and pointed down the street. She
couldn't quite hear what he was saying, but the thought
of what this wealthy couple would think if they knew a

little more about who they were talking to made her swallow a giggle as she meandered closer. Before the couple moved on, the young man shook Chaff's hand, thanked him with enthusiasm, and wished him a splendid day. Chaff wished them the same and watched them walk away for a few seconds before coming over to join her.

"You didn't—"

"Nick his wallet? Nah. Though it would have been easy as robbing a babe. It's a bit rum being taken for an upstanding gent like that," he stated with a bemused grin. "A bloke could almost get used to these flash togs."

"Go around talking like that and no one else is bound to make the mistake." She offered a teasing grin then gave a nod toward the least busy stretch of pavement leading away from the tower.

They fell into step together, heading off as though enjoying a pleasant stroll on a rare dry day. Shimmers of sunlight even broke through the cloud cover on occasion, like rays of hope, about as feeble as her chances of pulling this off. As they walked, Chaff leaned in close and spoke in a low voice, still managing a pleasant carefree smile and nod for anyone who met his eyes. Nothing to see here. Just an upstanding gent entertaining his lady friend.

"The bloke at the front desk told me, with many apologies to my esteemed client," he added, imitating the young front desk attendant with remarkable accuracy, "that Mr. Folesworth has been away for the better part of a week and isn't expected back for at least three more days."

That was as she had hoped and it was gratifying to

be right, though they had no guarantee that he was at the prison. It was at least a reasonable gamble. Thaddeus had a lot invested in the research and production going on at the new facility, mostly in the form of innocent lives taken, so he had good reason to spend a lot of time out there overseeing things.

"Brilliant. Now I just need to get up there and convince whoever is watching the place to take me to Thaddeus."

"If they don't put your lights out before you can open your bone box," he countered.

"They won't." *I hope.*

"Pigeon, I know from experience that I can't stop you doing a thing once your mind's set, but this is barmy on a whole new level. And please tell me you're not taking the cat."

"Macak," she corrected. "He makes his own decisions. Every time I try to leave him behind he finds a way to come searching for me. He's as likely to get hurt doing that as he is if I just let him come along." She watched a Lit officer scanning the crowd from where he'd stopped in front of the patisserie. His gaze didn't even pause on them. These flash togs were useful. "I have to try. Once Drake launches the attack with his battleship the chances of Garrett getting killed in the bombardment are too high."

"Are you doing this because you love Ash?"

She stopped and he stopped with her. When she turned to him, his blue eyes were full of trepidation, but the set of his jaw told her he was ready to hear the worst. She smiled and brought a hand up to touch his cheek. The time he'd spent in the prison with infection raging in his hand and arm had left his cheekbones more pronounced and put new shadows under his eyes. He would recover though. He already looked much better than he had when they brought him to Drake's manor.

"Not in the way your tone suggests. I do love him, but more like a brother. Certainly not the way I love you," her throat tightened as she added the last.

Relief took some of the tension from his jaw. He took her hand and kissed her palm, then he reached into a pocket and pulled out a strange little brass contraption that reminded her of the one Drake had been fiddling with the night he let her fly his airship. It was odd looking with so many tiny parts that she couldn't begin to make sense of it. She could feel her brow furrowing as she stared at it, waiting for it to declare its purpose. Nothing happened.

"What is that?"

He turned it over in his hand, his voice thick with unmistakable reverence when he spoke. "It's called the Allkey. It's a dandy little device Drake invented. It can open any lock."

"I never heard anything about this."

"I found out about it a while back when I crossed Drake's path at one of the competing lurks in Cheapside. He was out looking for some boys to test the device for him at the time. I recognized it sitting on a shelf in his office yesterday and I thought it might come in handy for your little adventure, so I borrowed it."

She gave him a suspicious look. "Borrowed meaning you nicked it."

He shrugged and held it out to her. "I doubt he'll notice it. He's got bigger things on his mind right now and he had three others laying around the room. Besides, if he were a decent bloke, he'd have sent one with you just in case. You are heading to a prison after all."

"Fair enough." She plucked it gingerly from his palm, afraid it might break if she were too rough with it. "How does it work?"

Chaff stepped in closer, helping to shield the object she held from prying eyes. His nearness also made her very aware of how he smelled like the soap from the manor and yet still with that hint of leather and dust that she associated with life on the streets. She wanted to step into his arms and stay there until the world simply went away. This was probably the craziest thing she had done in a while, which was saying a lot considering some of the things she done. Nothing she did to prepare was going to make it safe, but this might help her chances, if only a scant bit.

"You put this little metal rod into the lock and then flick this open to free the mechanism. It'll do the rest."

She nodded. The parts of the device looked so delicate she was almost afraid to breathe on it.

"Tuck it away somewhere safe. You don't want them taking it from you."

She stood considering for a moment, then realized that, while she didn't have much in the way of a chest, she was wearing women's clothes and there was enough there for her to hide something this small. She drew out a thin lady's kerchief from a pocket and wrapped the device then moved up against him, using him as a decency screen, and discreetly tucked it in under her bosom.

Chaff raised his brows and gave her a scoundrel smirk. "Need me to check and make sure it's secure?"

"Thanks. You're a real gentleman, but I think I've got it." She gave him a teasing glower.

He held his hands up in surrender. "I'm only trying to help."

Dressed as they were—and with Drake bankrolling the endeavor—they were able to find a restaurant to seat them for a nice early dinner. They'd gotten a suspicious eye from the waiter until Chaff explained that she was his parent's ward and he was merely looking after her while her parents were at a society party. They enjoyed a splendid meal, but Maeko couldn't shake the uneasy feeling that it might be her last. At least it was a good one with someone she loved.

Dark fell while they chatted and dined and she snuck nibbles of food to Macak to keep him appeased in his satchel. Once or twice, when intervals between bites went longer than he felt they should, a soft meow would emerge from the satchel and she would laugh quickly as though Chaff had said or done something humorous to throw off anyone who noticed the odd sound coming from their table.

All too soon, dinner was over, the restaurant was behind them, and Maeko found herself tucked into the shadows of a street corner with a view of the back entrance of the Tower, Macak draped over her shoulders, purring contentedly. Chaff squeezed her hand.

"You sure about this, May?"

She poked him hard in the ribs, knowing he was

mispronouncing her nickname to distract her from the weight of the moment and willing to play along.

"Ouch." He rubbed at the spot, smiling good-naturedly. "I deserved that."

"Yes, you did… and no, I'm not, but this is the best idea I've got."

"Want me to keep Macak?"

She gave him an appreciative smile for at least calling the cat by his proper name.

"No. Like I said, if he wants to come, he'll find a way. Might as well just take him with me and save him the trouble." She scanned the nearby rooftops and the windows of the top suite, looking for anyone who might be watching. "Keep an eye out until you see me leave with them, then get word back to Drake."

"What if I don't see you leave with them?"

She ignored the question. "It should take you about as long to get back to the manor as it will for us to get to the prison. If I can't get to Captain Garrett within 12 hours, I probably won't be able to get to him at all."

"Be careful, Mae. We'll meet you at the rendezvous point in the prison. If you can't get Garrett at least make sure you make it there. You can't save everyone."

She turned to him and kissed him once then put a hand to his cheek and smiled.

"I can try." It was time to go now before she lost her nerve. "Ganbatte, my love."

He caught her hand. The dim light of a gas lamp highlighted the lingering gauntness in his face from the ravages of infection, making him appear almost skeletal. It reminded her how close she had come to losing him completely. "I love you, Pigeon. I expect you to come back to me."

She nodded, afraid to say anything.

He let her hand slip out of his. "Ganbatte."

CHAPTER TWENTY ONE

T he Airship Tower was visually no different than it had been when she lived there briefly with Lucian except that, where it had been a place of haven then, it now felt hostile, as though the walls themselves were eager to expose her to her enemies.

Last time she had been captured. Nearly drowned by Joel and Bennett. The memories did nothing to soothe her nerves. Then, as so many other times before, Chaff had saved her. It was a wonder he could stand to watch her walk into this place again. That he trusted her to try this at all made her chest ache.

He really did love her. She could see it in his eyes and feel it in his touch, recognized it in the trust he gave her. How had she missed it before? More mysteriously, how had she missed those feelings in herself?

Macak nudged her cheek and she nodded. Now wasn't the time to be wasting ticks of the clock pondering over such things.

Her gaze moved up to the windows of the top floor. Lucian's flat. There was a single light on, shinning dim through one window. Lucian's study, if she had her bearings correct. She hadn't seen anyone looking out that window, but someone was up there. Bennett or Joel, perhaps. As much as Bennett scared her, she almost felt like he would be more inclined to hear her out than Joel would. Thaddeus would listen to her, which made a powerful argument for waiting until he was here, but he was more apt to give in to her demand to see Captain Garrett if they were already at the prison when she made it.

She could picture him in her mind, Lucian's twin, sitting in Lucian's chair, sleeping in Lucian's bed, his vile fingers digging through Lucian's things. Her gut filled with black sticky gobs of hate. Lucian might have done awful things to Macak, things she wouldn't have been able to forgive had she known about them when he was alive, but he was still a better man than his brother.

She made her way to the door in the back of the tower that she had used a couple times before. So far, she hadn't been caught coming in and out that way and she knew the lock mechanism well. When there was no one around, she hurried to the door and placed an ear to the crack, already putting her lock picks to work while she listened. She wanted to try the Allkey, but it was well hidden and there was a good chance they would search her for lock picks. When they found these, they would take them away from her, but they would be less likely to continue searching once they had that set. Better to let them take the picks.

Macak pushed his head in, tucking it under her chin and cocking it to the side as though he were listening too. She smiled and finished with the lock, scratching the cat's head as she inched the door open and crept inside. As soon as the door was shut, Macak leapt down, slinking low along the wall a few feet ahead of her, his ears twitching to and fro to catch any warning sounds. They were a third of the way across the big room when the cat froze so still that she almost lost sight of him. Something moved in the darkest shadows of the corner near the door into the lobby. Her heartbeat jumped to a gallop.

A figure stepped out from the wall. "Hello, little rat." *Bennett.*

A few seconds ago, finding Bennett first had seemed a good plan. Suddenly she didn't feel so comfortable running into the hired killer first, not in this dark room with no witnesses.

Maybe she'd misjudged him. He reached out and flicked a switch on the wall. The sudden light stung her eyes, but his would have to adjust as well. They both blinked in the light, then she noticed the large knife he held unsheathed in his right hand.

She glanced at the door behind her. Could she outrun him?

Bennett's game grin told her he didn't think she could. "I didn't think you'd have the nerve to show your face around here again, but this isn't the first time you've surprised me, is it?"

"I need to speak to Thaddeus."

Bennett smirked and took a couple of long, sauntering strides toward her. "I seem to recall him not wanting to talk to you again if you didn't meet his deadline."

"I think he'll change his mind."

He touched his fingertip to the point of the dagger as though testing its lethality while he swung his leg around in another exaggerated, lazy stride forward.

"Seems you need to change my mind first."

Somehow those few long-legged strides had eaten a substantial chunk of the distance between them. She moved one leg back, ready to pivot and run.

"You'd make your boss very happy if you brought me to him with my new offer."

He chuckled. "That'd be a sound contention, if making the boss happy were my biggest concern, but I'm not really the loyal, devoted lapdog type."

She shifted her weight on to the back leg.

He sheathed the knife then, and she almost dared to relax a little until he drew out a pistol and her skin flushed with the heat of renewed fear.

"How 'bout I just shoot you here and leave the mess for the Tower staff to clean up?"

Macak bounded out then from where he had been hidden alongside the wall and leapt up to her shoulders so suddenly she nearly cried out in surprise. The cat bumped her cheek with his head as he took up his usual place there then turned to stare at Bennett with his raised pistol as though daring him to take the shot. Bennett's reaction was unexpected. The killer cocked his head to the side a fraction, staring back at Macak for a minute or more in silence, then he lowered the gun.

A broad grin cut across his features.

"I beg your pardon. Looks like your life is already spoken for." He sheathed the gun and gestured for her to come over with a wave of his hand. "Thaddeus isn't here right now," he said in a conversational tone, as though talking to an old mate and not someone whose life he had threatened mere seconds ago. "Let's go see if Joel's up for a ride out to the prison."

Maeko stood up straight and stared at the man, certain he'd gone mad, or madder in his case. What just happened?

Bennett had turned away and was walking toward the door now. He opened it and stopped there, holding it for her. He actually looked confused by her hesitation. "Come on then."

Puzzled, she walked over and stepped through the door, a shudder of dread sweeping through her then coiling in to form a cold lump in her stomach as she moved past Bennett. He followed through after her, waving off one of the guards when the man started in their direction with a look of alarm.

"All under control," Bennett called, guiding her to the lift. Then, aside to her, he remarked, "Ever notice how animals are much better judges of character than we are?"

She absently scratched Macak's head. Was that it? Were they mates now simply because she had the companionship of a cat? Life was unfathomably odd sometimes, but she wasn't about to argue with a bit of good fortune.

"You like cats?"

"Better than most people," he answered. "They're clever, manipulative, handsome little beasts, and quite efficient killers." He reached out to give Macak's head a scratch.

She resisted the urge to step away so he couldn't touch the cat. Macak, it seemed, knew what he was doing almost better than she did.

"So, you're not going to kill me?"

He gave her a sideways glance. "I can if you'd like,

but I'd be loath to deny this fine fellow his companion. It's clear he's picked you."

Good thing I let you come, mate. She gave Macak a quick scratch under the chin.

"You have an odd code of ethics."

Bennett smirked. "I'll do most anything for a bit of tin, but I try not to cross crows and I always respect the turf of my fellow clippers."

"You're equating cats with assassins?"

He gave her a sideways glance. "You saying they aren't similar?"

As if to support Bennett's postulation, Macak extended his lethal little claws, pricking her shoulder lightly. She'd never seen Macak kill anything, but she'd seen plenty an alley cat taking down mice, rats, and birds in the unfriendly back streets. They were efficient hunters and she'd seen a few better fed felines kill without eating their victims after, so perhaps it made some sense that he regarded them as kindred creatures in some convoluted way.

"What now?"

"We go see Joel."

"Why? Couldn't we just get in a coach and head out to the prison?"

Bennett was staring at Macak who stared back quite calmly, as though he still felt it necessary to keep the man in his place, which it probably was. "Nah. Much as I despise the bludger, Thaddeus left him in charge."

Maeko felt her gut drop with dread as the lift slowed to a stop. Bennett slid the door open and gestured for her to proceed him out. She could smell fresh bread when she stepped out into the landing. Were

Lucian's servants still there? She couldn't imagine Joel making bread, but that was what it smelled like. Too fresh even to have come from the bakery across the street. This was the smell of bread baked in house.

She stopped before the double doors, reluctant to face Joel. Bennett continued past her, opening the door and walking in first this time. She could run now and abandon the plan. He was giving her that option and, despite how little he knew her, he somehow seemed to know she wouldn't take it. She couldn't give up now. Taking a deep breath, she walked through the door he left standing open for her.

As soon as she was inside, she found herself facing another brandished gun. Joel had been sitting on the sofa with his feet resting on some of Lucian's science journals strewn carelessly across the table. He swung his feet down, knocking some of the journals on the floor, and stood, drawing his gun and training it on her before she was fully through the door. To her not-so-secret delight, as displayed by her smug grin, Joel also found himself facing down a gun when Bennett drew his own pistol in her defense.

Joel's face went red so fast she almost expected him to blow his top like an overfull teapot.

"What in the bloody hells is wrong with you?" His voice cracked as he shouted at Bennett.

"I've come to an agreement with the rat," Bennett stated, his posture and voice so relaxed she couldn't shake the feeling that he would kill Joel with little hesitation and even less remorse. "I told her I'd take her to talk to Thaddeus."

Joel's face was so red it was a wonder his skin

didn't ignite.

"Lucian," he shouted.

Bennett's shoulders rose and fell in a lazy shrug that reminded her of Reuben no matter how badly she didn't want to compare the two men in her head.

"It isn't as if she doesn't already know the truth."

A figure moved a few inches into the doorway from the kitchen. Constance. Her eyes were circled with dark shadows of sorrow and fatigue, her mouth drawn in a tight line of stress. There was a smudge of something down the front of her dress and her hands gripped her skirts in tight fists. She spotted Maeko, refusing to meet her eyes, and turned back into the kitchen. That meant she knew as well. What price kept her silent?

Maeko yearned to talk to her, but she had more important things to accomplish. Constance was on her own for now. If things went in favor of the Pirates, she'd probably be looking for new work before long.

"It doesn't matter," Joel snapped in his usual pleasant manner. "If you don't use the right name all of the time, you're more likely to slip up when it matters. Thaddeus has to have told you this at least fifty times."

"*Who's* told me that?"

Bennett snorted a laugh as Joel burned brighter still. So bright Maeko thought a red light could probably be seen shining out the windows from below. Only the twitching of his finger over the trigger stopped her from laughing as well.

"Lucian," Joel hissed through gritted teeth, "doesn't want to talk to her."

"I think we'd best let him decide that."

Joel stared at the pistol pointed at him, his pistol

still aimed at her. For a few seconds, he appeared to be pondering options, but finally came to the same conclusion she had. Even if he and Joel were on the same payroll, the hired killer would have no qualms about pulling the trigger that his finger rested so easy on. Joel lowered the gun.

Bennett kept his gun raised a moment longer, waiting until the nose of Joel's weapon was sliding into the holster. Then he lowered his as well, though he didn't holster it yet. "I'm glad we agree. Let's get a move on. This place bores me."

T he coach ride was long and silent, though Joel's anger somehow created an intense sound pressure in the small space. Maeko sat uncomfortably on the bench beside Bennett because she refused to sit next to Joel. Macak curled between them. Though she appreciated the buffer, she had to bite her tongue to keep from telling Bennett to keep his hands off her cat. If Macak created a common ground between them that kept her alive, then she needed to let the cat continue working his magic.

She had managed to spot Chaff in the crowd across the street as they were leaving the Tower. He'd given one quick nod, waited for her almost imperceptible return nod, then hurried off toward where Drake's coach would be waiting. The tightness in his lips and the distress in his eyes was obvious even from a distance. He hated watching her go with them, possibly even more than she hated going with them, though she at least had the limited comfort of knowing Bennett had come to her defense once. Whether he would do so again remained to be seen, but it was a small bit of hope to help bolster her courage.

The silence of her companions left her only time to think. Chaff and Ash had come to her to apologize at the urging of Drake. She didn't doubt their sincerity. What she didn't understand was Drake. Was he simply what he claimed to be? Did he want no more than to fight for the oppressed after having lived among them for several years as an outcast to his own family? He had asked for the rest of the blueprints if she could get them, and his reasons for doing so were sound. There could be useful technology in some of those designs that might have other applications. It would be shameful to let it go up in flames or, worse yet, stay in Literati hands. However, she had no solid proof that Drake wouldn't put that technology to similar use once the Lits were thwarted, assuming the Pirates came out on top.

None. She had no proof. She would just have to trust her instincts if she even got the opportunity to seize the blueprints in the first place.

If she did succeed in rescuing Garrett before the Pirates attacked, what then? Once they were clear of the prison, what was the next step? Would she go to Whitechapel with Chaff? Would she continue rebuilding her relationship with her mum? Would Drake ask her to continue working with him and the Pirates? What of Amos? Would he go on with Em's work? Would she help him if he did? What about Ash? Would she see him again, or would they go their separate ways? So much was uncertain, but one thing was certain: she was keeping Macak.

She stroked the cat's soft coat, avoiding his chin where Bennett was currently scratching him, not wanting to make any kind of contact with the hired killer.

At least some decisions in life were easy, though she had to make sure nothing happened to Macak, and they were heading to a place where bad things were apt to happen.

I'll protect you, mate.

That cat turned his head almost as though he had heard her thought. His big yellow eyes met hers and he blinked once, slowly, as if to say he would do the same for her.

When she glanced up, she found Joel glaring at her. She scowled back at him, silently wishing his face would get stuck in that unflattering expression, before turning to stare out the window until the coach rolled up to the outer wall of the prison.

They were admitted through the gates as soon as Joel leaned out the window. The coach pulled around next to one of the many buildings. Joel was up and climbing out before it had come to a full stop. He slipped a little when his feet hit the ground, but, much to her disappointment, he managed to right himself and stormed off toward the door of the building, leaving her with Bennett. He vanished inside without a backwards glance.

"He's an insufferable blighter," Bennett remarked casually.

Unable to argue, but not sure how much rapport she could bear to develop with him, she climbed out of the coach in silence, Macak hopping out to trot along dutifully beside her. She marched into the building ahead of Bennett. No point dallying at this juncture. There was only so much time and it was going to pass quickly. They had already consumed a good hour, maybe more, getting to the prison. That left less than 11 hours to go before Drake made his move.

This building was different than the one she'd gone into to find Chaff. That building had been dedicated more to medical use. This one had a lot of rooms that looked like offices, at least in the front section.

"Left turn," Bennett directed from behind her when they came up on a crossing hall.

Maeko glanced to the right, spotting rows of cells at the far end of that hall. The hall to the left was its mirror, with a wall of cells at the far end. Before they made it more than halfway, a door toward the end opened and Joel leaned out. He vanished back inside after he spotted them coming.

"That room I suppose?" She inquired.

"Lead on," he replied in somewhat vague confirmation.

Maeko drew in a deep breath and went to the room. She opened the door, walking through without missing a step as though she had no fear. That trembling jelly feeling in her lower gut was nothing. Nothing at all. No more than the cold sweat on the back of her neck.

Thaddeus was seated at the head of a long table looking over some paperwork. Two thuggish blokes stood flanking him as though concerned for his life in the presence of a slender little half-Japanese street rat. Joel had taken a seat a couple of chairs down from him. Maeko chose to walk down the opposite side of the table until she was standing across from Joel, facing Thaddeus. Bennett walked around to the side Joel was on, stopping almost behind him.

"I didn't expect to see you again after you broke

that boy out of here," Thaddeus remarked, not looking up from the paperwork. His tone offered no insight into his temper.

"I rather hoped you wouldn't, but things change."

Thaddeus did look up when Macak leapt up on the table behind her, his eyes tracking the cat as he jumped from there to her shoulders.

Joel sneered. "That's appropriate, two vermin banding together."

Bennett leaned down close to Joel's ear and said in a dangerous tone, "Cats aren't vermin."

A shudder of unease swept through Joel then and Maeko couldn't quite hide her smile.

Thaddeus didn't look amused. "Don't go thinking he's on your side, Rat. Bennett's only loyal to the tin that fills his pocketbook."

And cats.

She nodded. "I figured that."

"Has anyone searched her?" Thaddeus asked the room at large.

Bennett shrugged and glanced at the long table between them. After a moment's hesitation, he stepped up on a chair and walked over the top of it. Using another chair to step down on her side. All the while, Thaddeus looked like someone was scratching their fingernails down a chalkboard. Maeko appreciated the irritation he caused his boss. She appreciated less the upset his action caused Macak, who dug in his claws in deeper than usual. She winced inwardly, refusing to let Thaddeus or Joel see her pain.

She braced mentally for what was sure to be an unpleasant experience, but Bennett was very professional about the process, making no uncalled-for investigation, though some of what he avoided would have borne fruit. He started at the bottom, quickly finding the lock picks she expected them to find as well as the small dagger tucked in by her other shoe. Both items she'd planned to lose. He searched the satchel she was carrying as well, but it was only for Macak and therefore empty at that moment. He tossed the lock picks and dagger on the table and turned to face Thaddeus.

Thaddeus gave a nod of satisfaction and met her eyes. "Why are you here?"

"I did get Chaff back, but he blames me for what happened. The Pirates don't trust me, and they're getting people hurt. I don't want to be a part of what they're doing and I owe them no loyalty. I have no reason to stay there now."

"That's quite the sad tale, but it doesn't explain why you'd come here."

"Ash is the only one who has stood by me and I don't want anything bad to happen to him. He said he would leave the Pirates with me if I could find a way to make sure his dad is all right. So here I am, ready to trade information about the Pirates for a chance to speak to Garrett."

Thaddeus narrowed his eyes. "If they don't trust you, what information could you have for me?"

"I can't give you their location, but I know of a rendezvous going on at half three tonight. If you go there and follow them from the rendezvous, they'll lead you back to the stronghold."

Thaddeus cocked his head to the side and

considered her with cautious interest. "Where is this rendezvous?"

"I'll tell you after I've talked to Garrett."

Thaddeus smirked. "I'm not that daft. I need to know you aren't lying before I let you anywhere near my prized engineer."

Maeko's gut twisted. Truth be told, she hadn't expected him to go for it, but she had dared to hope. It would be a lot easier to get Garrett out of here if she knew exactly where he was in the facility. Wells had given her a good visual of the layout and where he thought Garrett was being kept, but if he was wrong, she could waste all of her time searching for Garrett and trying to dodge security. Now she would have to hope for the best. At least they hadn't taken the Allkey.

"I've a question for you," Joel piped up. His smug tone didn't bode well. "Have they finished their battleship yet?"

Maeko hoped she didn't go as pale as she suddenly felt, though she had a relatively white complexion to begin with, so maybe they wouldn't notice. How did they know about the battleship?

"I didn't know they were building one," she answered, hoping her pause wasn't long enough to garner suspicion.

Thaddeus waved a dismissive hand at his companion.

"It doesn't matter now. We've got the weapons to take it down." He focused on her then, and it was all she could do to keep a straight face. "Tell me exactly where the rendezvous is. I'll have some of my men investigate while you wait here in a cell. If you're telling the truth, when they get back I'll take you to talk to Garrett, then you will be dumped outside the walls and I'll have you shot if you try to get back in. If you're lying, we'll skip directly to the shooting part."

"Not the best deal," she grumbled.

"It's the best I'm going to offer. You already turned down my good offer. Be happy I'm willing to give you this much."

After a few minutes of deliberation, she gave him the location of an old warehouse she and Chaff and some of his other pickpockets had often used as a meet up point when they had to scatter from the Lits. "They should be there no later than half three in the morning."

"Well enough. You better not be lying and you'd best behave yourself while you're my guest." He nodded to Bennett. "Lock her up."

"What about the cat?" Joel asked, giving Macak the most unfriendly of smiles.

Thaddeus scowled at Bennett. "Let her keep it. It won't hurt anything."

Joel's face fell.

Maeko was too anxious to gloat. She only had so much time and so much information to go on. And if they already knew about the battleship, if they already had weapons to fight it, did the Pirates stand any chance at all? They needed to know, but she had no way to get back to them until Chaff and Ash arrived to pick her up. By then it would be too late to stop the assault.

CHAPTER TWENTY THREE

The young man they had left guarding the cells looked at least as young as Ash. He held the gun they had given him like it was some sort of trophy of adulthood, brandishing it about alarmingly as he strolled around the cell block with an unconvincing swagger. The boy was scared half out of his wits. She could see it in his twitchy movements, the way his jaw worked when he wasn't speaking, and rapid blinking of his eyes. It made her even more uncomfortable with him waving his weapon around. Macak sat on the hard cot bathing one foreleg. Far less concerned about their increasing odds of being accidently shot than she felt he should be.

"What's your name?" She inquired, wincing when he startled and almost dropped the gun.

"I ain't supposed to talk to prisoners."

She gave him an easy smile. A hard feat given the weight of time bearing down on her and the intense desire to duck just in case he fired unintentionally. "You just did, didn't you? And nothing awful happened."

"Course not, but that's because no one saw."

She suppressed a smug grin. "Are you sure no one saw?"

"Yeah. I'm the only one working this block till

noon tomorrow. Only security in this building at all right now. Ain't no prisoners here but you and you ain't all that worrisome."

That was beautiful to hear. At least she had a chance of getting out of this building relatively unharmed if she could simply get rid of him.

"That's an awful long shift. Don't they ever let you rest?"

"That's a neat cat," he said, ignoring her question and pointing at Macak with the dangerous end of the gun.

She must have tensed visibly because he blushed and lowered the gun.

"Sorry. He is pretty neat though."

"Yes. He is." She thought she might have to ask again, but after he had stared in fascination at the cat for a few minutes he turned back to her.

"I'm Travis. I was a prisoner, but they gave me a good deal for out time and three meals a day if I work security. The shifts is long, but it ain't so bad." He blew a lock of blond hair out of his face and offered a smile that made him look younger still.

He turned then as though he meant to make another walk around the block.

"You can pet him if you want."

Travis brightened and walked over to the edge of her cell. "Just so you know, I ain't got the key. They don't trust me that much."

That didn't surprise her. He was a prisoner after all. The bars were much too close for her to squeeze through so the Allkey would have to do the trick.

She picked up Macak, ignoring his protest at having

his bath interrupted, and took him over to set him down beside the bars. Travis met her there, keeping his gun half trained on her with one hand as he squatted down to pet the cat. She squatted down as well, waiting until his hand was stroking Macak's soft fur and his face brightened. Then she darted her hands through, grabbing his gun hand and pulling it far enough in to crack his wrist bone hard against the bar. His grip faltered and she snatched the gun, turning it on him as he yanked his injured hand to his chest.

"Blood and ashes! I think you broke it!"

"I'm sure I didn't," she countered, already working her hand into her top to get at the well-hidden Allkey.

"I told you, I ain't got the keys." He had backed up a few steps, his lips pursed in a dramatic pout.

"Travis," she started, keeping her tone gentle, "I just need to get out of here."

His pouty look turned into one of puzzlement and something that might have been a hint of alarm as she dug around under the blouse with her one hand. When she finally pulled out the kerchief and unwrapped the Allkey awkwardly with one hand, he was approaching the bars again, forgetting the weapon trained on his head.

"What's that?"

"Back up," she warned and he gave the gun a wary glance as he moved back again. She reached through to feel around the lock until she found the keyhole and slipped the tiny rod into it, then flicked the mechanism. A soft whirring sound made her want to watch what was happening, but she didn't dare get distracted. A few seconds later, the lock clicked, freeing the door.

Travis watched her step out of the prison cell with something akin to awe. "Where can I get one of those?"

She stepped away from the cell and gestured with the gun for him to go inside.

His face fell. "Oh no! I'll get in so much trouble if they find me locked in there and you gone."

"Tell you what. You get in there. I'll go find what I need to find, then I'll come back and give you the Allkey before I go." She felt bad lying. Still, sometimes you just needed to do whatever it took to move things along.

He looked suspicious. "Why would you do that?"

"Because you seem like a nice chap. Besides, you don't have a lot of choice. I'm just trying to sweeten a bum deal."

His weary nod told her he realized she was right. He walked into the cell and stood back while she closed it. Then she used the Allkey again, delighted to discover that it would indeed work to lock the cell the same way it had unlocked it. She smiled at Travis and lowered the gun. "Hang in there, mate. It could all work out in your favor." *If we don't all die in some terrible explosion.*

"Sure it could," he replied dubiously. "Will you bring back my gun?"

Maeko hesitated, staring down at the hateful thing in her hand. If only he knew how much she would prefer to let him have it back right now. She could leave it here. There was no law saying she had to hold on to it now that she had it in hand. Then again, she was going wandering in the stronghold of a man who wouldn't blink an eye if she ended up dead for her efforts. Even those here who didn't know her history could bring her a great deal of grief. Armed, she at least had more than her wits and the hope that they might have a soft spot for cats to bargain with.

When she looked up, she saw Travis watching her. There was something in his eyes at that moment that told her he wasn't as daft as he seemed. He nodded, his expression serious.

"Do what you want with it." He averted his gaze then. "Just be careful."

In that moment, she wanted to let him go and take him out with her. He would only increase the chances of getting caught though.

"I'll come back if I can." It surprised her some to realize that she meant it.

He glanced at her, a little of her surprise reflected in his eyes. "I actually believe you mean that. Go on. You're wasting time."

You have no idea.

Without another word, she discarded her cumbersome skirt to move about in the much more functional trousers and struck out, doing her best to remember where she would find the door that would put her closest to the building she was looking for from the map Wells had modified. He'd done a fine job. She'd have to tell him so if she ever saw him again.

Macak moved slightly ahead, pausing at every door and crossing. She let him take point, knowing his senses were tuned more finely than her own. For all that she was a rat, he was a cat and, as much as she hated to agree with Bennett, there were few who could claim to be better hunters than a cat. When she had found him, he'd been with the grisly remains of his most recent rodent kill, after all. His metal leg was almost silent with little pads built into the paw much like the real ones. The whir and click of the gears was whisper soft.

When they got to the exit, she plucked Macak up and tucked him in the satchel. Maeko felt a twist of guilt at his single meow of protest.

"Sorry, mate. You're an invaluable ally, but I'm not risking you on a venture with these odds. When Chaff and Ash get here, they'll find you and take you out of this place." At least that was what she hoped they would do. If she wasn't there when they got to the rendezvous spot, but the cat was, they would hopefully understand that things were riskier than she liked and return to the airship where they could wait safely to see if she returned with Garrett. That sort of sensible behavior was probably too much to hope for from those two, but it was worth a try.

She turned out the electric lights nearest the door, took a deep breath, and cracked the door open. Her eyes lit upon the glint of a light reflecting off something metal on someone's boots and she almost pulled the door shut again. Some part of her brain registered that the boots were moving away and she paused. The figure, mostly hidden in darkness, was heading away from this building. If she struck out now, it should be a while before he came back around.

Holding her breath, she pushed the door further open, wincing when it squeaked once. The guard was too far away to hear it, though it sounded like a scream in her ears. Her pulse was racing. She peered about for any sign of other patrols, then she stepped out and inched the door carefully shut, her nerves twitching with the need to move on. Sticking to the shadows as much as possible, she darted around the side of the building. When she got to the next building, she started toward the wall, toward where the boys were supposed to meet her, then stopped and ducked back next to the shadows of the building.

There was a guard up on top of the wall. He'd paused there for some reason and she held her breath again. Had he seen her? The last thing she needed was someone on the wall to see her and raise the alarm. She stood still as a statue and waited. A spattering sound reached her ears and she grimaced. After a few minutes, he did up his trousers and turned her way. His eyes skimmed the darkness, seeing nothing in those deep shadows more because he didn't expect to see anything then because she was that well hidden. He moved on along the wall.

Either she had impeccable timing, or there were a fair number of guards wandering about. If it were the latter, Chaff and Ash might have a hard time getting the airship close enough without being spotted, but that was something they would have to deal with. She had no way to get warning to them of the guards or of the anti-airship guns Thaddeus claimed to have.

When she got around to the side of the building, she crept quick up the ladder there and deposited the satchel near the ladder tucked close to the wall. She regarded it then, hesitating.

What if something happened to her? What if Chaff and Ash didn't make it down? Would Macak be trapped here until he starved?

Maeko's heart ached at the thought of him suffering

and she picked the satchel back up, taking it down the ladder again. She put it on the ground by the ladder and loosened the fasteners a touch. Enough that, if he struggled hard, he could break free. At least here he wouldn't get hurt trying to get off the roof.

It was time to move on, but she hesitated again. She wanted nothing more in that moment than to pull Macak out of the satchel and clutch him to her. If she didn't go quick, she might lose her resolve.

"I love you, my furry friend," she choked out around the sudden painful tightness in her throat.

Clenching her teeth against the pull of tears, she turned and hurried around the side of the building to the next building down.

A dark door waited.

A door behind which she might find nothing good.

Maeko took hold of the handle. There was no way to know if anyone waited behind it. The metal doors and brick walls were too thick to let her listen through them. Instead, she pulled it open, one hand gripping the gun, and stepped inside.

CHAPTER TWENTY FOUR

M aeko hesitated, listening by the door after she eased it shut behind her. This was the last of the four smaller side buildings, closest to the two largest buildings. According to the map, this was where Thaddeus and other Literati officials had their offices. It was also where they had the prison cells for their more valuable *guests* like Garrett. There were also some sleeping quarters for prison officials and guards when they stayed at the prison for extended periods as well as a few rooms used for rest breaks and meetings.

The odds of there being at least one guard roaming the halls of this building were good. There was also significant risk of running into off duty officers here. Per Wells, the blueprints that weren't currently being developed were probably somewhere in Thaddeus's office. The rest might be in the research or production areas of the big buildings. If she didn't find them before she found Garrett, he might have a better idea. If the blueprints were in the big buildings, she wasn't going to go after them, especially if she managed to get Garrett out first.

Where she entered should be close to the Lits sleeping quarters. It was late enough that there was a chance anyone who happened to be in there might be asleep.

She heard footsteps and tucked herself into the nearest doorway. The door was open, the room dark. Numerous beds and a few tables and chairs occupied the space. Moving the rest of the way in, she pressed herself against the wall alongside the door and nearly jumped out of her skin when someone snored loudly beside her. She pressed a hand over her mouth to quiet her startled breathing and slid down the wall into a crouch, listening over the breathing of the guard next to her to try and pinpoint the guard in the halls.

The sleeping guard was snoring loud enough that she couldn't hear the footsteps. Or perhaps the patrolling officer had moved out of earshot, but she couldn't be sure. She gave the sleeper a cross look. Maybe, if she could get him to roll onto his side…

Maeko set the gun on a cabinet and crept over, pausing when his hand twitched. To avoid being seen, she lay on the floor and slid under the bed, then brought up one hand and poked him in the side with a finger. There was a sudden snort and the whole bed jerked.

"Wha's who?" He muttered, still mostly asleep. The bed shook again as he shifted over on his side, snorted once, and muttered, "Bloody rats."

Indeed. This time she slapped her hand over her mouth to stop a laugh. *Not now*, she warned herself. There was a time for all things. Why was it that humor always found her at the most inappropriate times?

When his breathing evened out again, without the snoring this time, she slid out from under the bed and crept over by the door, collecting the hated gun along the way. She counted to sixty in her head twice, listening for sounds of movement out in the halls. She didn't hear the guard. He was still out there somewhere, but she couldn't stay in here and wait. She only had so much time to get this done.

Taking a deep breath, she moved out into the hall. There was no one in sight, so she continued to the first crossing. Once there, she listened for another sixty count, then leaned out enough to glance both directions. Right was clear. To the left, she spotted a figure walking away and ducked back fast, her heart racing.

How many times could she get lucky like that?

Jammy dodger, Chaff's voice said in her head.

She smirked and peeked out again, spotting the figure's boot heel as he vanished around the far corner.

No time to waste.

She darted out and hurried to the left, stopping at the first door on the left of that hall, the one that should lead into Thaddeus's office here. Pressing her ear to the edge to listen, she counted to sixty again before she turned the handle and pushed it open. The room was dark. A nicely furnished office with several file cabinets and a large desk along with a fancy, well-stocked cellarette against one wall. It was an office she could see Thaddeus using.

Quick as a cat, she skimmed through the desk and the cabinets, finding what she wanted in the second cabinet. She pulled out the blueprints, suddenly wishing she had Macak's satchel to put them in. With a little extra searching, she found a briefcase tucked curiously in behind the cellarette and popped it open. It had some paperwork in there that she ignored, piling the blueprints in and crushing it closed.

Now what?

She couldn't carry the case around while she was hunting for Garrett, but she was still close to the exit. Perhaps she could tuck the blueprints somewhere near the door.

How much time did she have left?

Maeko ducked back out of the office, her heart in her throat. The guard could be anywhere. Nerves prickled like knives along her spine as she padded back to the sleeping quarters and tucked the case behind the cabinet by the door. That done, she moved back into the main hall and turned left at the intersection again. Right would be faster according to what she remembered of the map, but it made sense that the guard might be following a consistent route around the building, in which case she'd be more likely to run head on into him if she went to the right. Her plan assumed that he was the only active patrol, but this part of the prison didn't have that many prisoners in it, according to Wells. As long as too much hadn't changed, there was a good chance they wouldn't be wasting manpower putting extra patrols in these halls.

She made her way around through the halls to the back corner of the building where there was a run of better furnished cells, with thick mattresses on the cots, as well as actual mirrors and sinks. These weren't cells for regular criminals. They were cells for the Lits special guests. The first two were empty and didn't look as if they'd been used at all yet. The third was occupied by a stocky man with arms thick as her whole body. He was sitting on the cot staring at his big hands when she padded into view.

For a long moment, the man stared at her with a furrowed brow as though wondering if he were hallucinating. Then he stood and hurried to the front of the cell.

"Who are you? How'd you get in here?"

Maeko put a finger to her lips, glancing toward a hallway that intersected this one a few cells down.

He lowered his voice. "You have to let me out of here."

She looked him over. He could be an innocent victim like Garrett. He could just as easily be a dangerous criminal who had some skills that earned him a better place in the prison.

"Why are you here?"

"I've been assisting Garrett. Doing the heavy lifting for his assembly work the most part."

Looking at the bulging musculature under his shirt, that was easy to believe. It also didn't exonerate him of any possible criminal status. In fact, with a plethora of prisoners to choose from, being strong wasn't the kind of skill they would have had to go recruiting for.

"How'd you get in here?"

He folded his thick arms and scrutinized her. "You the judge?"

She scowled back at him. It wasn't so scary with the bars between them, but memories of Hatchet-face sent a little shudder through her.

"I'm a small female trying to execute an improbable rescue alone in a prison full of people who would be happy to see me dead. I can't afford to be cavalier about this."

He gave a soft chuckle. "I can't argue with that

logic. What do you want to know?"

"What will you do if I let you out? Will you fight for the Lits?"

His immediate glower was enough of an answer, but he also said, "I'd never fight for those blighters."

"Will you hurt people?"

His eyes jumped up and he tensed as another voice spoke behind her.

"You really don't know when to quit, Rat."

Maeko spun so fast she almost fell over her own feet. Her gut dropped to her knees as she trained her gun on Tagmet.

He raised his own gun. "How in the bloody hell did you get in here? No. I don't care. I'm more interested in how you think you're going to get out. From where I'm standing, your odds don't look so good."

Maeko moved back, keeping her gun level as he followed her forward into the hall. "You don't have to do this. You let me go once before."

There was something almost like pity in his grimace. His eyes said he might regret what he was about to do, but he would still do it. "I'm not a nice man, Rat. I haven't got much in my life. My wife died five years ago. Now all I've got is my job and I believe in doing my job right. Once, I failed at my job and let you and those worthless Pirates get away. I've been kicking myself every day since then. I will not fail to do my job again."

She couldn't shoot him. Even if her conscience didn't reject the idea of shooting anyone, there was the added complication that a gunshot would wake the other guard. But Tagmet didn't know she knew about the other guard. As long as he didn't know she knew about the other man, he might believe she would use the gun. Of course, he could always tell her about the other man.

Almost as if he'd followed her train of thought Tagmet smirked at her gun. "You don't want to shoot that. You'll draw out the other guards in the building."

Guards plural? Was he bluffing, or did they have more company than she realized. She glanced to the prisoner who gave a small shake of his head and held up one finger.

Tagmet lunged toward him with the gun and the prisoner flinched back, his eyes narrowing.

"You aren't irreplaceable, Hugh," Tagmet growled in warning.

Something flashed in the prisoner's eyes, a hatred so intense that Maeko caught a shout of warning on her lips as he lunged in turn, his thick arm darting between the bars with a surprising fluidity. He caught Tagmet's wrist in a grip so strong that the Lit officer dropped the gun and reached for his hand, his face twisting with pain. He had no time to do anything else before he was jerked into the bars with a clang of impact that made her wince. Then Hugh twisted him around, wrapping one arm around his throat and pinning him against the bars.

Tagmet's eyes started to water. His face turned red, a lump already rising on his head from the impact with the bars. Maeko lowered her gun and started toward him, not quite sure what she meant to do. She stopped when he lashed out at her with one desperate hand.

"Please, Hugh," Maeko said softly. She used his

name to appeal to his humanity. "Please don't kill him."

The prisoner's strength showed in how easily he kept the officer pinned there despite his struggles. He gave her an irritated grimace.

"Why the bloody hell not? He'd have killed you, and he's taken more than his share of pleasure in tormenting those of us on the wrong side of the bars."

"Please," she repeated, remembering in vivid detail the officers who died when she freed Hatchet-face. "There is enough blood on my hands."

Tagmet's struggles were growing weak.

"This blood wouldn't be on your hands girl."

"It would though. He never would have been so careless if not for me."

"That was his mistake, not yours." Something in his eyes softened though and he clenched his teeth as though the decision he was about to make distressed him. Tagmet fell limp against his arm and the man immediately released him, letting him drop with an unceremonious thud to the floor. Maeko stared at Tagmet for several seconds until she saw the faint rise and fall of his chest.

She nodded and looked at Hugh with a measure of sincere gratitude. "I need to find Garrett."

He gestured down the hall with one hand. "He's in the luxury suite at the end of the row."

They regarded each other for a long scrutinizing moment and Maeko glanced from the cell lock down to Tagmet and back again.

"Tell you what. Let me out and I'll act as your bodyguard until you're out of this place."

"Then what?"

"If we get out alive, I'll go find my daughter in Norwich and see about finding some honest work."

"Swear?"

He nodded. "Been meaning to get straight for a long time, but the money they were offering was too good to pass up. Almost died last time, though. Would have if the Lits hadn't broken things up." Hugh paused, perhaps considering the irony. "I'm done with that work."

Maeko took out the Allkey and set him free.

M acak had almost struggled his way free of the satchel when someone moved it from outside. After a bit of fumbling, it opened and he found himself looking into the face of one of Her boys. The taller one with the lighter hair. Chaff, She had named him. The boy didn't look all that happy to see Macak who, for his part, was rather uncharacteristically chuffed to see him. Help had arrived.

"Where's Maeko?" That was Her other boy, the younger and shorter of two. Ash. The one she seemed less inclined to mate with.

Macak stepped out into the open and peered up at his rescuers. They weren't the most inspiring saviors, but they would have to do.

"She isn't feeling very optimistic about her chances if she left the cat behind."

"Macak," Chaff corrected. Macak didn't know many of their sounds, but he recognized his name and rubbed against the boy's leg in appreciation. It was encouraging to see that one of them could be taught. "We need to find her."

"But where do we start?"

Whatever they were chattering about, it was time to intervene. They needed to find his girl and they needed

228

to do it fast. Hostility hung over this place like a thick London fog and somewhere, his girl was swimming through it. These two weren't nearly as good at communication as She was, but they were all he had to work with.

Macak made the leap, instinctively making special calculations for his metal leg, and landed on Ash's shoulders. The boy startled so violently that he couldn't stick the landing, but he'd expected some reaction along those lines and managed a decent landing back on the ground. When he looked up, he thought Chaff might have been shot the way he was doubled over with one hand on his gut and the other pressed over his mouth. But the shorter boy's incensed look and the humor radiating off Chaff told him something entirely different was going on. His tail twitched with a fresh spark of impatience.

"That wasn't funny," Ash grumped.

Chaff moved his hand from his mouth, sucking in a deep breath to get control. "Oh, yes it was. You jumped like you'd been shot."

"Out here, it's a real risk. I think Macak is trying to tell us something," Ash said, his tone sullen. "You think he could show us where she is?"

"Well, he's found her before with worse odds."

Both boys turned to stare down at him. He stared back at them, tail twitching a bit faster now, and meowed.

"All right mate, we're counting on you. Show us the way." Chaff gestured toward the building.

Macak didn't hesitate. Human speech was a garbled mess, but the gesture was clear enough. He turned and struck out around the building, following the tracks that smelled most recently of Her, moving slow and careful, wary of their many enemies. As a cat, it wasn't all that hard to go unseen and, even when he was seen, he was oft ignored, though he couldn't count on that here. Now he had followers to consider. If his girl was in trouble, as She often was, he might need these two, if for no other reason than to open doors, so he needed to keep them intact long enough to get Her out safe.

He was pleased to find that the boys took things seriously. They'd fallen silent and were keeping their postures low and alert as they followed him. Ash didn't move with the almost catlike fluidity that Chaff did, but Chaff was a creature of the wild streets. Like Macak himself, he'd grown up needing to be unseen more often than not. Ash had learned much in his time with the girl, but he was still a domesticated creature. He was strong though, and he cared deeply for Her, so he made up in those traits for what he lacked in street proficiency.

When they got to the door, the lanky thief crouched down next to it, placing one hand on Macak's back as though to keep him still while he cautiously turned the handle. For a second, Macak was tempted to move away from the presumptuous touch. It was comforting though, in a moment when his little belly was wound in knots of fear for what might happen to his girl. She'd been awash with sorrow and dread when She left him. He knew those feelings. She didn't think She would be coming back. But She was his and he was Hers and he wasn't going to lose Her now. It had taken too long to find Her.

He sniffed the air coming from the building when Chaff cracked the door open. He could smell Her. He could smell others too. Angry others, drowning in their own malcontent. They stank and two of them he had smelled before. He and the two boys would have to be extra careful here. She was most definitely in danger though, so they would have to split caution with haste.

They moved into the building together. Macak started to move ahead, then stopped. There were two others nearby. One smelled of sleep. He could hear the snoring to confirm it. The boys were waiting, watching him. He cocked his head toward the sound of the snoring and Chaff mimicked the movement, holding a finger to his lips in some signal to Ash. After a moment, he nodded and pointed toward the doorway just ahead of them.

"Someone's sleeping in there," he whispered to Ash.

Satisfied that they were aware of the danger, they began moving, walking as soft as they could in their boots. Macak led the way, the stench of a familiar foe stinging his nose. His hackles began to rise the closer they got to the crossing hall. The foe was in that hallway and he wasn't moving. He was waiting. Waiting for Her perhaps. Waiting for them if he had heard them enter. He stank of cruelty tinged with anticipation.

Macak stopped moving and the boys stopped as well.

How was he supposed to warn them about an enemy who wouldn't betray his presence?

He stared up at Chaff who was closest, hackles up and tail twitching madly. Chaff looked down at him and he glanced to the right, the direction in which their foe waited, then up at the boy. Chaff stroked the fur down on his back, his smile full of a dreadful understanding. He pulled his left arm awkwardly in close to his chest, his hand in front of his face, and nodded at Macak. He then made a few gestures to Ash, hand held up flat followed by three fingers. Ash nodded. Chaff stepped out into the hallway.

Several shots rang out, intermixed with the clang of bullets striking metal. Ash ran out into the hallway then and Macak went with him. There was a whirring and clacking sound and suddenly a gun was poking out of Chaff's left sleeve, trained on their opponent who had his own gun pointed back at them out of his own false arm. It was the man She had named Hatchet-Face, though the metal arm was new.

Hatchet-Face sneered at them. "You're not who I was waitin' for."

In his other hand, he was holding a briefcase.

"You're not who we were looking for, so I guess we're even," Chaff answered.

Ash inched closer and Hatchet-Face shifted his gun. He set down the briefcase and drew a second weapon from under his ratty jacket. Ash stopped moving.

"You're not a Lit guard," Chaff observed.

Macak moved over by Ash's feet and sat, ready to react in a moment's notice. This was not his area of expertise, however. These were the affairs of humans that went on above the head of a cat. For the short term, he would wait to see how things unfolded. He could sense the unpredictability in their opponent. They would all be better off if he didn't move around too much and irritate the man.

"I'm the hired help. Let out of my cell for good behavior." He smirked and Macak suspected that, if the dreadful man had a tail, it would never stop twitching. "Hired to keep things in order. I don't recall you being part of that order."

"We don't want any trouble," Ash offered.

Hatchet-Face chuckled. "If that were true, you wouldn't be here."

Macak stood and pressed into Ash's leg, trying to draw his attention to the sound of someone approaching from behind them. It was too late to do much of anything about it though. The gunshot had woken the sleeping man.

"Welcome to the gathering," Chaff said, turning slightly toward the newcomer, though he didn't move his eyes off of Hatchet-Face. Macak agreed with him on who was the greater threat, but the new man also had his gun out, trained on Chaff.

"What's going on here?"

"You folks must be rather desperate for recruits, fitting a cracked bludger like him with a gun," Chaff said, still talking aside to the new man.

"Wasn't my decision," the new man answered.

Whatever he'd said, it was the wrong thing. Hatchet-Face narrowed his eyes and moved one of the guns. Another shot fired, deafening in the small space, making all of them jump. Behind them, the new man's eyes widened, red blooming at his throat. He dropped his gun and toppled, making a few wet choking sounds before he fell silent. Red began pooling around his head and shoulders.

The fear coming from the boys increased, thickening the air around them. In the silence that fell, Macak heard the faintest sound of breathing coming from a side hall behind Hatchet-Face. He lifted his nose to the air, detecting the faint scent of three more individuals. One was unfamiliar. Another he hadn't smelled in some time. The third he recognized with a delight that settled his fur and turned his tail to twitching for an all new reason.

Hatchet-Face looked at the man he had killed and shrugged, smiling at Chaff. "I guess you were right about me. Who's next?"

A bludger every bit as big and intimidating as Hatchet-Face stepped around the corner. Something caught Hatchet-Face's attention, perhaps a shift of someone's eyes, and he turned, swinging the gun that had been trained on Ash around behind him. Ash didn't hesitate. The moment the gun was moved, he sprinted in, lunging and grabbing Hatchet-Face's arm. He managed to twist the wrist of his hand enough that he dropped the gun.

His girl entered the hall then and Hatchet-Face broke his arm free from Ash while he swung the arm with the built-in gun around, not toward Ash, but toward Her.

Macak sprinted in and leapt, catching hold of the flesh arm and digging in with claws and teeth. He tasted blood and hatred and vengeance. Hatchet-Face roared and shook the arm hard. Macak quickly began losing his grip. The bludger swung his arm and sent Macak flying, but not before he left long bloody runnels in his flesh. Macak twisted, hitting the wall feet first and bounced away, twisting again to land neatly on all fours. He looked back in time to see Hatchet-Face's other arm, the metal one with the gun, swing out. He caught Ash a solid blow to the face with one meaty fist. Blood sprayed through the air as Ash spiraled away and slammed into the wall.

One shot rang out, or perhaps two at the same time. Hatchet-Face jerked where he stood and turned to face Her, wavering in place as he raised the gun. Another shot rang out and he jerked again. The arm with the gun dropped a bit then came back up. Another shot. Hatchet-Face staggered closer to Her. His eyes burned with loathing. He leveled the gun at Her again. Pure rage and hatred keeping him on his feet. Macak bunched and leapt.

Maeko stared at Hatchet-Face, knowing that the loathing in his eyes was mirrored in her own and hating him even more for making her feel it. The gun leveled at her and time stopped, his finger tightening on the trigger. Then Macak leapt up and latched himself onto Hatchet-Face's back. The man bent backward, letting out another roar of pain, his shot going wild. He flailed with his other hand, trying to strike at the cat now attached to his back. While he thrashed about, bleeding from several gunshot wounds, Hugh grabbed the wrist of the mechanical hand and stepped into him, slugging him square in the nose.

Hatchet-Face dropped like a rock.

Hugh looked down at him in the frozen moment that followed, then back at her. "He's like to bleed out from those wounds before he wakes."

Once, she had helped Hatchet-Face get back into the world. It wasn't a mistake she meant to make again. She met Hugh's eyes and a cold lump settled in the pit of her stomach. "This time, I'll take the guilt."

"Dad!"

Ash's voice was muffled, one hand over his nose, blood running out between his fingers. Garrett ran past her over to his son. He pulled Ash's hand away from his face. Blood ran fast from his newly crooked nose.

"It looks like it's broken."

"I neber would'b guessed," Ash answered.

Chaff chuckled. "About time that pretty face picked up a little character."

Ash gave Chaff a cross look and flicked blood at him, though a pained smiled tugged at his lips. "Shuddup."

Macak leapt up into her arms then and she hugged the cat close, pressing her cheek to his head and squeezing her eyes shut. Her chest felt like it might explode. The gentle hand that touched her cheek a few seconds later didn't help.

"You all right, Pigeon?"

She opened her eyes and nodded, not trusting herself to speak.

Hugh walked over to Ash and his father. "This is going to hurt." He didn't give time for the words to sink in before he grabbed Ash's nose between his hands and cracked it back into place.

Ash cried out and reflexively punched Hugh in the gut.

The big man let out a small grunt and stepped back. "You're welcome."

"Thank you," Garrett offered, giving the man a fleeting glance that spoke of much shared guilt. Of things that they had done together here that neither wanted to talk about or be reminded of.

Next to the softly wheezing Hatchet-Face, who she hoped would bleed out soon so she didn't have to listen to that tortured sound much longer, sat the briefcase full of blueprints she had left in the sleeping quarters.

She stared at it. That he'd had it meant he must have seen her with it, which meant he must have been in the room when she put it in there. Had he been there when she hid under the bed, watching her? Waiting for the right moment to confront her?

Maeko shuddered and Chaff pulled her close against his chest, cat and all.

"Good work, mate," he said, giving the cat a scratch on the head. Louder, he said, "We've got Mae and Garrett. We need to get out of here and meet up with the airship before we run into more trouble or, worse, get bombed by our own people."

Maeko pulled back from him. "How long do we have until Drake and the others arrive?"

"Not long. He was itching to get going. He was worried that they might interrogate you and find out about the attack and he'd lose the element of surprise. I doubt he'll wait the full twelve hours he promised."

Garrett glanced over at them, the dread in his look confirming what Joel and Thaddeus had said.

She caught his eyes and held his gaze as she spoke. "They already know the Pirates are building a battleship. They've developed guns to take it down."

"Whad!" Ash's eyes widened, his shirt was painted with blood from his nose, though they had stuffed some cloth or something in his nostrils to try to stop the bleeding.

Garrett nodded solemn acknowledgement. "They do have the guns, but not all of them are functional. The two on the front corners of the wall are operational. After they finished testing the first two and were satisfied with the results, I designed a flaw into the next four so they would fail under the stress of firing. I knew they had plans to test the first two, so I had to make them functional. I was trying to appear cooperative given that they said they knew where my family was hiding out. I couldn't take the chance that it was true."

"Ad leasd id's only doo," Ash offered.

"But two of those guns functional is enough to take down any battleship that doesn't know they're there," Hugh added. "They also have a mobile gun, but I don't believe it's functional yet."

"Can we disable themb?" Ash asked.

"We have to," Maeko answered. "We have no way to warn the battleship before it gets here, especially if they're planning to move in early."

Garrett looked away then. He heaved a sigh. "She's right. We can't let them fly into those guns. Hugh and I know where they are and how to disable them. We can take care of that and meet back up with you three somewhere."

Hugh was nodding as he spoke, but Ash shook his head vehemently. "I amb nod leabing you. I jusd god you back."

"We'll have a better chance if we go in small groups," Maeko stated before Garrett could voice the argument in his eyes. They didn't have time for a standoff of stubbornness. "We'll split up and meet back at the rendezvous when the guns are disabled."

Chaff gave her forehead a quick kiss then turned to the others. "Ash, you and your dad go to the one on the near corner. You're injured, so you shouldn't be expected to go too far."

"You were shod," Ash argued.

It wasn't until then that Maeko noticed the three bullet holes in the arm of Chaff's shirt. Her gut did a spin.

He looked at the holes and grinned. "Metal arm," he answered cheerily. "Hugh and I will go for the far one. Maeko will take Macak back to the airship and let Crimson and Wells know what's going on."

"Oh no," she protested. "I'm not leaving you four to do all the dirty work."

Chaff turned to face her, hunkering down to look her in the eyes.

"You've done enough already. Macak needs you and the two in the airship deserve to know what is going on. Besides, they might have to do an emergency pickup if things get rough. Trust me," he mussed her hair, "you'll have plenty of opportunity to get into more trouble."

She glanced past him at each of the other three. Three sets of eyes stared back at her, unyielding. Even Hugh had taken his side.

"No. Chaff, I…"

He stopped her with a kiss, his lips soft and full of sweetness and warmth. "It's our turn, Mae."

She swallowed hard, feeling the sting of tears. Her arms tightened around Macak, but the cat made no complaint. He only purred louder.

"Id'll be all righd."

She released a shaky breath. "I expect you all to make it to the airship in one piece."

Chaff smirked. "That'd be an improvement over last time."

"You want this back?" Hugh held Travis's gun out

to her.

She shook her head, managing not to recoil visibly. "No. You'll probably need it more than me."

Chaff took her hand then and she let him lead her toward the exit with the others, grabbing the briefcase on the way past and leaving Hatchet-Face to die next to the officer he had killed.

At the door, they left in pairs. First Chaff and Hugh, who had the farthest to go, after she kissed Chaff once more and made him promise to be as safe as possible. Then, a few minutes later, Ash and his father struck out after she gave Ash a tight hug. Lastly, she and Macak stepped out into the darkness and started creeping toward the building that they were supposed to meet the airship on top of.

Travis was still locked up in that building. Perhaps she should go in and set him free. If he was still in the cell when the attack started, he wouldn't be able to get out of harm's way. Besides, no other patrols had been in that building. It would almost be safer to pass through there then to walk around outside where a wall patrol might spot her.

Holding Macak close, she veered toward the near door of the building and ducked quickly inside. She waited for two counts of sixty beside the door, listening for any new sounds that might suggest additional company. All she heard was Travis whistling a lively tavern tune from back in the cell.

She smiled to herself. He might turn into a decent bloke given the right opportunities. Hugh was working out and that was why she was here, wasn't it? To give the youth a chance at something better than this. That and the fact that it seemed safer to go through here than stay out there. She already knew what to expect in here.

She hadn't quite taken a full step when the door swung open behind her and something struck her across the side of the head before she could finish turning around. Macak flew from her arms and she hit the ground, tasting blood in her mouth as her teeth slammed home on her tongue. Her ears rang so loud it took a few seconds before she even realized there were now people standing over her and speaking.

"Don't kill her, Joel," Thaddeus warned, much to her distant appreciation. "We need to find out where Hugh and Garrett are and how she planned to get out of here with them."

Someone grabbed a handful of her hair and started using it to pull her to her feet. She grabbed their hands, trying to help lift to get relief from the sudden pain.

"Bennett, go raise the alarm."

When she was on her feet, she finally managed to look around, determining by his absence from view that Joel had been the one to pull her so ungently to her feet. Bennett still stood by the door, not rushing off to follow his orders. He was looking at Macak who was crouched a few feet away with his hackles up.

"Blood and ashes, man," Joel snapped. "It's only a cat."

"It's a killer," Bennett murmured. "A kindred spirit."

"You can keep the blasted thing if you like," Thaddeus offered, "so long as it doesn't make a nuisance of itself before you get back and you do as you've been ordered."

Bennett met her eyes then, and she longed for some

reassurance in those cold eyes. Anything that would promise her, at the very least, that Macak would be all right. There was nothing. No emotion at all that she could find in those bottomless pits. Her chest tightened as he glanced once more at Macak and went back outside.

"We obviously have some urgent matters to discuss," Thaddeus remarked, staring hard at her now. "Bring her along, Joel."

"What about the cat?"

Thaddeus glanced at Macak who laid his ears back and hissed.

"Feeling's mutual," he answered. "Grab that briefcase. I'm sure the wretched cat will follow her. Come along."

With that, he started further into the building and Joel discouraged her thoughts of dissent by prodding her in the back with his gun.

CHAPTER TWENTY SEVEN

D o you know who founded the Literati?" Thaddeus asked as he led the way into a small office.

Maeko was rubbing the side of her head where Joel had struck her. She spat blood to one side, finding a small pleasure in how much it stood out glaringly red on their nice sterile white wall.

"No. And I don't really care."

Thaddeus sat in a seat behind the desk and gestured for her to sit in the only other chair. For a moment, she considered refusing out of sheer defiance, but she was feeling a touch woozy, so she sank into the seat, leaving Joel to stand off to one side. Macak hopped up into her lap, but didn't settle there. He stood staring at Thaddeus and Joel in turns, perhaps trying to decide which posed more of an immediate threat.

Thaddeus leaned his elbows on the desk and steepled his fingers.

"I'm glad you asked," he resumed, not at all discouraged by her lack of enthusiasm. "One of the queen's most trusted advisors was involved early on naturally, though he didn't take much interest beyond serving his primary purpose of getting the queen to approve of Literati activities. Initially, it was intended to be strictly a scientific community comprised of inventors wanting to brainstorm their ideas with likeminded fellows. An idea championed by none other than the late Lucian P. Folesworth and a young talented inventor from a wealthy family that he'd taken a fancy to, one Dominic Rakeley."

Her attention perked up a bit, though she took care not to show it. Dominic Rakeley. A young inventor from a wealthy family. D. Rakeley. Drake? Could it be? It would explain a lot.

"Of course," Thaddeus continued, "as it grew, the organization started gaining political clout and some of the members began pushing their own agendas. There were those who wanted more influence in the city. They wanted a way to force their inventions into production and public consumption. They were looking for a way to control the populace they needed to consume their work. That was how the Literati police force was born along with several other discreet arms of the Literati that would extend influence in other ways. The queen's advisor remained involved only as far as he was needed to convince her to avoid taking too much interest in their expanding activities.

"The Literati quickly grew out of the scope of its founding ideals. When the original vision appeared to have become lost before the ambition of some of its members, Dominic was the first to extricate himself. Lucian followed his example soon after. Although he continued to provide some funding and ideas, he refused to be involved in their heavy-handed tactics. When it became clear that Lucian was no longer going to share any of his remarkable inventions with the community and that his company was going to be taking away from the consumer pool they wanted to monopolize, they approached Joel to find another way to get their hands-on Lucian's inventions and his share of the riches. Unfortunately for Lucian, he wasn't willing to come around on the subject, so Joel called on me to brainstorm some more extreme options. Soon after that was when you came into the picture, I believe."

She spat some more blood from her oozing tongue onto the desk, and Thaddeus leaned away, eyeing the spot of red with disgust.

"What does all this have to do with me?"

"Your detective friend. Ah, late detective friend," he corrected with a look of mocking sorrow, "was stirring up some trouble through the Bobbies. Trouble we thought we'd put down when we took care of Commissioner Henderson and my brother. With the detective out of the way, things were looking up and victory was all but assured. Now, thanks to the right ears in the right places, we know we should be looking up quite literally.

"The Pirates, it seems, must have at least one very wealthy individual working on their behalf who can afford to fund a battleship. Needless to say, a battleship attacking this facility would draw quite a bit of attention we don't want at this juncture. Throughout these recent complications, you've caused our organization more trouble than one small girl should even be capable of, especially tonight. But we will find Garrett and Hugh. My men will come back from your supposed rendezvous in Whitechapel and report that it was all a lie. Then things will settle down again. However, they won't stay that way unless we can stop this battleship from paying a visit.

"So what does all of this mean for you?" He leaned further back and put his feet up on the desk. "It means that, unless you want to watch Joel gleefully skin that cat alive for practice before he starts on you, you need to tell me where the Pirates are building that battleship."

Maeko smiled in the moment of expectant silence. She didn't feel like smiling. She felt like heaving. But she smiled instead. "I don't hear an alarm."

Thaddeus's face went red, his eyes narrowing as he realized she was right. He pulled out a gun, training it on her, and glanced up at Joel. "Go see what's going on."

It was only a brief reprieve. The instant Joel was out the door, Thaddeus turned his attention back to her and she didn't have an answer to give him. She could tell him where the stronghold was, assuming that the Pirates would arrive soon and take out this facility and the majority of the Literati's power base with it, but then, what if they failed? There were too many people at Drake's estate who would suffer. And she could see by the look in his eyes that she had already hesitated too long. He wouldn't believe anything she said now.

"I can't tell you where they're building the battleship."

Thaddeus lifted the gun. "I guess that's it then. It appears that you are of no use to me."

There was a loud boom from somewhere behind Maeko, in the direction of the large development building near the back of the prison. Seconds later, another explosion shook the building they were in and Maeko cried out, throwing herself to the floor with

Macak clutched tight in her arms. For perhaps a minute, she wasn't sure if Thaddeus had fired or not. She held her breath, waiting for pain. What came was another explosion and a crack split the ceiling of the room, dust raining down on them.

The first explosion had come from the back of the facility, which meant the battleship had approached from behind. Now that she thought about it, that was probably the smarter approach. Just as people never tended to look up for danger, they also tended to expect it to come from in front. It might also give the others time to disable the big guns before it got into range. However, it also meant guards would be running for those big guns, which put the other four in significant danger.

Another explosion, this one hit somewhere away from this building. Maeko looked to one side and met the eyes of Thaddeus who had also ducked down by the desk. His eyes narrowed, hatred blazing bright in them. Still clutching Macak with one hand, she jumped to her feet and lunged for the door, throwing it open on a cloud of smoke and billowing dust. She grabbed the briefcase by the door with her other hand and sprinted into the maelstrom. This time the shot did fire.

A burst of pain in her side made her stagger, almost dropping Macak, who was none-too-pleased with being slung about like a sack of meat as it was. He twisted and broke from her hold, running ahead. Maeko kept after him, not slowing down to see how bad the wound was. It was a flesh wound. At least she was determined to believe that. It hurt like the blazes. Her head felt a bit floaty as though she'd had too much laudanum, making it hard to focus. A sudden wave of nausea didn't help the situation.

Macak stopped to wait for her on a pile of rubble at a crossing hall, barely visible through the smoke and dust. When she reached the hall, she looked down toward where the cells were, but most of the building in that direction was collapsed, dark sky visible through the haze where the ceiling should have been.

Her chest tightened. *I'm sorry, Travis.*

One thing was certain, they wouldn't be rendezvousing with the stealth airship from the top of this building.

Macak hissed and she followed his gaze, glancing behind her to see a figure moving in the haze. Pain took her breath away when she started moving again, but she couldn't stand here and wait for Thaddeus to finish the job. When they got to the door, she shoved it open, letting out a cry of pain when the motion pulled at her wound and fresh warmth ran down her side. Tears squeezed from the corners of her eyes, but she ran from the building with Macak sprinting alongside her. Death was a great motivator and Thaddeus would be her death if he caught her now.

Fires lit the night. There were screams of pain and shouts from those running to help or to fight. A sudden explosion ahead made her stop, ducking into the shadows of the next building to get her bearings. She stood panting, every breath agony in her side.

The last explosion had been the front gate of the prison, but it had blown inward, which didn't make a whole lot of sense if the battleship, invisible in the dark night amidst billows of smoke and dust, had hit it. They most have had something else out there to blow the gate in. Another explosion tore into a building near the front and the burst of flame illuminated figures streaming in through the front gate. Pirates for certain, but some appeared to be wearing uniforms, though she couldn't make them out in the brief flash.

The wall she was standing beside exploded outward then and she was thrown in the air, losing sight of Macak in the blast. She hit the ground hard, pain bursting through her injured side. For some time, she could only lay there, her ears ringing, unable to think a single coherent thought. When thought returned, there was only one word in her head.

"Macak!" The shout came out cracked and hysterical sounding. She struggled up to her hands and knees, discovering new pains as she moved, though none so piercing as that in her side. "Macak!"

She got to her knees then struggled to her feet, tears streaming down her cheeks as much from the pain as from fear that she had finally lost the cat.

Another figure was getting up several feet away. Thaddeus stumbled once, shook his head, got his bearings and stood. He started walking toward her then.

Pain, fear, hatred. She stared at the approaching figuring, watching as he lifted his arm, still holding his gun.

"You lose, Thaddeus," she snarled. "No matter what you do to me now, you still lose."

His arm faltered, started to sink as he looked around. Then he refocused on her, his face twisting in an awful sneer.

"Maybe, but you won't live to see how it all works

out."

She stared down the gun and all she could do was hope someone found Macak. Hope he was all right.

The loud crack of a gunshot split the air.

CHAPTER TWENTY EIGHT

Maeko flinched, expecting agony.

Thaddeus cried out and crumpled, falling to his knees clutching the hand that had been holding the gun. Maeko looked around and spotted Chaff walking up, the gun in his arm still extended. She sucked in a shallow breath. He was alive and had saved her life yet again.

The relief couldn't overshadow her other fear. She peered into the dust and smoke around the rubble that had been the wall of the building.

"Mae," Chaff called as she sprinted past him, the pain in her side flaring fresh with the movement.

She stopped in her tracks when another figure began to emerge from the haze. Lean, lanky, and tall, with fluid movement like a cat. She shook her head, watching with expanding dread as Bennett emerged from the smoke and dust. He had his arms pulled in to his chest and, for a second or two, she thought he might be clutching an injury. Then she saw the fur and her heart stuttered in her chest.

Macak!

Forgetting who held the cat, she ran over to him.

Bennett held Macak out to her. The cat seemed to hang there for a moment, listless and dazed. A bit of blood matted his fur in a few places. Then he lifted his head, looking at her, and meowed. She took him in her arms and held him tight, clutching him close despite the searing pain as cloth pulled away from the wound, causing more bleeding in her side. Tears of relief streamed down her cheeks. By the time Chaff reached her side, Bennett was gone again.

She became aware of the others still approaching from the direction of the gate. When they passed through lit areas, she recognized some of them as Pirates from the stronghold, but there were others with them wearing distinctive uniforms now that she got a better look. Bobbies. Odd how a weight lifted off her chest when she recognized those uniforms. Uniforms she had feared before the Lits pushed them out of London. Those uniforms meant Amos had succeeded on the groundwork Em had laid with them. They meant the Bobbies believed that the wrong brother survived the airship explosion. They meant the Bobbies believed her, which had to be a first, and they were working with the Pirates.

A low rumble drew her attention away from their allies then. She and Chaff turned as one to see a large door lift open on the side of one of the big buildings. Men with an array of large guns, some as part of false appendages, streamed out around a massive machine. It looked almost like a large rectangular coach. The sides were fully enclosed in heavy looking metal with slits in a few places where windows might have been. Instead of wheels, it had six triangular appendages, three on each side, on which the tread, but not the center, rotated. Toward the top center of the moving metal box was a long barrel of certain purpose. As they watched, the long barrel angled upward and the box itself turned so the barrel was pointing toward the battleship that was coming around for another pass.

All of a sudden, the barrel sparked to life at its base, then crackles of bright lightening danced up along it in rapid stages until it hit the end and a projectile flew up through the air. For a few seconds, lightening continued to dance across her vision. When the image briefly burned into her vision cleared away, she saw the battleship still in the sky and thought that perhaps the gun had failed. Then the front of the battleship began to drop from the sky, swinging down toward the front corner of the wall where Ash and Garrett had gone to disable the gun. Chaff was already back, and he'd had further to go, but that didn't mean the others hadn't run into trouble.

She glanced at Chaff. "Where are Ash and his dad?"

Chaff shook his head. "I don't know, but we have our own problems." He pointed ahead.

Whoever controlled the battle coach appeared to consider that task done and the dramatic sinking of the battleship emphatically supported their assessment. The main barrel lowered and two side panels opened, putting out two slightly smaller, more traditional guns. The accompanying gunmen and the coach itself were turning their attention toward the invaders coming through the front gate, the ones behind her and Chaff.

Thaddeus was still bent over his damaged hand. They would have to leave him to be found by whichever side reached him first. If they didn't move now, they were going to be caught in the crossfire.

Chaff touched her arm. She met his eyes and nodded, then followed him at a low sprint deeper into the rubble and the concealing dust that had swallowed Bennett moments ago. Macak struggled a bit now. She didn't want to put him down just yet though. He had blood on his fur in places and she had no way of knowing how badly he might be injured.

They stopped and crouched in some rubble to get their bearings. She winced with every breath, nauseated and dizzy with the pain in her side.

"Do you know where the little airship is?" She asked, watching the battle coach approaching where Thaddeus was now standing, clutching the wounded hand out in front of him like some diseased thing.

"It saw it move outside the wall when the gate came down. There was nowhere safe for it to stay once the battleship move in." He looked at her and his eyes narrowed. "Are you all right?"

With Macak in her arms, he wouldn't be able to see the blood soaking the side of her clothes. That didn't mean he wouldn't notice the pain in her face. He'd known her too long for her to hide that.

"Just a scratch."

His eyes narrowed further. "Let me see."

"Blood and ashes, Chaff. Remember those bigger problems you mentioned? They're still getting bigger."

As she spoke, the battle coach opened fire with the two side guns. They shot at remarkable speed and range, taking down several Bobbies and Pirates before the remaining invaders sprinted for cover. Over the wall, people were diving from the falling battleship with parachutes. She could only imagine Drake's fury in that moment, watching his prized warship going down after one short, albeit destructive, pass over the prison.

"I need to get in there."

Maeko almost jumped from her skin when Ash spoke behind them, jerking hard enough that pain stabbed through her side, eliciting a gasp and making her lose her grip on Macak. The cat landed graceful at her feet, still quite agile despite his roughing up in the explosion. He crouched at their feet, watching, ready to partake in whatever plans they devised.

"Middle of a battle is not a good time to be sneaking up on folks, mate," Chaff snapped, obviously as surprised as she was by his arrival.

Ash grinned. There was no cloth in his nose now, but still plenty of blood drying down his shirt. "You're just sore I managed to sneak up on you."

"Where's Garrett?" Maeko asked.

"He went out to the airship. He's going to take it up for a better vantage and to look for a place to drop in to get us. He sent me in to find you two and it's a good thing he did. Looks like we've got some work to do. They can't bring the ship in with that thing in here and it's going to destroy our people."

Chaff met her eyes and they both nodded. That infernal machine had to be stopped quickly if they were going to hold onto any advantage they'd gained though the surprise attack of the battleship.

"What if we go around behind?" Maeko suggested. "They're focused forward right now. We'd only have to take out the two men in the back. Chaff and I can do that. If we get you a clear path, can you get in there and disable it?"

Ash nodded. "I think so."

She looked at Macak, his fur a mess with dust, debris and some blood. "Don't suppose I can ask you to stay behind?"

The cat's bright eyes held hers for a few seconds. He shook himself then leapt up to her shoulders.

"I figured as much," she muttered under her breath, though she couldn't deny the way his weight on her shoulders lightened her spirits and gave her just a little hope. She glanced at the others. "Let's go."

Keeping low, they made their way around the intact portion of the building. As they came around the side in the dark, she glanced at the next building down. Somewhere in there was Travis, though from the looks of things, the section he was in was naught but rubble now. Perhaps, if the Pirates survived this mess, they could try to find him. He might still be alive in there. If not, his blood was on her hands too.

Mixed with my own.

She put her hand to her side, feeling how damp the cloth of her shirt and jacket were. There was a constant severe pain there with frequent sharper jabs of pain accentuating her movements. She couldn't stop and worry about that now though. No matter how it hurt. No matter how nauseous or lightheaded she felt, they had to stop the battle coach. With the battleship out of commission, the Pirates and Bobbies didn't have a weapon that could take it down.

Keep going.

There was shouting and shots being fired. When they got around the back of the building they could see that the gunmen with the coach had ducked into cover, exchanging occasional fire with their opponents. Mostly they were waiting. The coach turned and lowered its center cannon. Lightening arced along its length again and a slug shot out. It hit a block of debris some Pirates were hiding behind and shattered it, breaking it down and giving the gunmen a chance to fire as the Pirates bolted for new cover. One of them took a shot in the leg and went down. When another turned back to help, he was shot in the chest and dropped where he was. The one with the leg wound started dragging himself, but didn't get far before another gunman's shot finished him off.

The nausea in her gut spread, not from pain this time.

There were only a couple of men near the back of the battle coach. One on each side. Chaff gestured to himself then pointed to the far one then to her and the near one, who was also conveniently shorter than the other.

She nodded. "Ganbatte."

Chaff smiled solemnly. "Ganbatte."

Ash smirked. "What you said."

Chaff moved out and back, Ash moving with him. No one was watching behind them with the fight raging ahead. Maeko set Macak on the ground and grabbed a chunk of stone. She waited a few seconds until Chaff was in position. Then she moved up behind her mark.

Her heart was racing faster now, which wasn't at all helpful with her injury. Glancing over, she saw Chaff rising behind his mark, lifting his metal arm up to make the blow. She took a deep breath, regretting it for the flare of pain, but she channeled the pain into anger and swung the stone with all her might, striking the man behind the ear as hard as she could.

A wave of conflicting guilt and relief swept through her when he dropped to the ground. She glanced over to see if Chaff had succeeded, and her eyes caught on someone stepping past the far side of the coach with a gun raised. Ash sprinted into her vision as the man Chaff had gone after started to turn around. Chaff's blow hit, but it hit the wrong spot, knocking the gunman off balance as he spun back toward him. Chaff grabbed the big gun the man was swinging around, trying to wrench it away. Several shots fired, most of them still aimed toward the battle ahead. The man stepping around the battle coach, however, had fired back. Ash staggered, but the shot hadn't been a killing one, perhaps only because the shooter was Thaddeus, firing with his off hand. Wherever he'd been hit, Ash didn't slow long, lunging into Thaddeus and taking him to the ground.

Maeko looked around. The coach and the rest of the gunmen were still advancing. Both boys were locked in struggles of their own. She lacked the mechanical knowledge Ash had to disable the machine, but there was another way to stop it. Because of the guns mounted in the sides, the door in was on the back of the metal box. Grabbing the gun from the man she had downed with one hand and digging for the Allkey with the other, she sprinted for the door.

CHAPTER TWENTY NINE

Always willing to take a chance on good luck, she tried opening the door when she reached it. It was locked. The coach was moving slow enough that she could press close and maneuver the Allkey. The key again lived up to its name. There was a satisfying click and she opened the door.

There wasn't much time to think. The sudden change in the air and in the noise in the interior of the coach drew the driver's attention. Joel slammed his foot down on a lever and grabbed for the gun lying near his hand. Maeko spared a second to shut the door behind her and flip the lock. She lunged forward, but wasn't fast enough. Joel snatched up the gun and his hand was suddenly wrapped in a glove of fur and teeth and flailing claws. He let out a high-pitched shriek and slammed the hand and cat into one wall of the coach. Macak lost his grip with the sudden impact as Joel flung him into a back corner. He hit hard with a clang of metal on metal and dropped to the floor.

"No!" Maeko screamed before terror and the force of her rage took her breath away.

She was close enough now, with the time Macak's attack had bought her, to grab Joel's hand. His hand was slippery though with the blood the cat had drawn,

260

so she dug her fingernails into a deep scratch for grip. Joel cried out. The pain left him reeling and vulnerable. Following his example with Macak, she slammed his wrist into a corner of metal three times in rapid succession. He dropped the gun.

Maeko started to bring up the gun she was still holding, but Joel wasn't ready to be defeated yet. His eyes lit, and before Maeko could react, his other fist plowed into her wounded side. Her breath went out and she crumpled to her knees. Joel brought his knee up and she turned her face fast enough that he caught her in the cheek rather than the nose, but the blow still knocked her back on her tailbone.

Joel grabbed her hand now, twisting to get the gun free of her grip. Maeko sucked in an agonizing breath and spotted opportunity. Releasing the one gun, she rolled to the side near Macak and grabbed the gun Joel had dropped. She swung it around and they both fired. The shots were deafening in the enclosed metal coach. They stared at one another. Then red blossomed across Joel's chest and Maeko waited to feel the blossoming of her own pain. It wasn't pain that she felt though. It was warmth. The warmth of a small warm body on her chest. A small, warm, unmoving body.

Horror dawned on her and she fired again even as Joel was starting to collapse. The second shot caught him in the side of the face, twisting him around so that he fell across her legs.

Maeko dragged herself out from under him and lay Macak on the floor, her chest twisting into knots. His little metal leg was twisted, the front panel torn half off. There was blood in several places, his fur such a mess that she couldn't tell how much was his.

"No. Macak," she almost couldn't talk around this pain, so much worse than that in her side. "You're not allowed to leave me."

Tears were already flowing when she pressed her cheek gently against his chest. Then she heard it. A quick feline heartbeat. His chest began to rise and fall slightly against her cheek and a small, querying meow emerged from him.

Crying harder now, Maeko choked out a laugh, though it turned into a groan with the pain in her side. Joel's punch had started the bleeding again. Someone pounded on the door.

"Maeko!"

She got up and flipped the lock. Ash and Chaff rushed in and slammed the door shut behind them. She reached over and locked it again. Ash's hurried to the front, his left arm hanging at his side, the sleeve soaked with blood from his shoulder. Chaff was ineffectually trying to stop the blood flowing in a stream from a gash on his head.

"We need to scare these blighters into submission," Ash snarled, turning the battle coach.

It only took him a few moments to figure the machine out, then he fired the side guns, blasting a round at the gunmen to their right. He missed, but she got the feeling he wasn't actually trying to hit anyone. They scattered, running in panic. Someone tried to get in through the back door with little luck.

Unlike a traditional coach, there were no seats for passengers in this monstrosity. Maeko cradled Macak gently in her arms and sank down on the floor. She leaned against the wall, breathing shallowly to limit her pain. Under different circumstances, she might have tried to help the boys with their injuries, but they were doing as well or better than she was and Macak needed her.

Chaff grimaced at Joel, then he ripped a sleeve off of the dead man's shirt and pressed it to his wound before going forward to offer Ash directional guidance.

Maeko kept one hand where she could feel Macak's heartbeat. "We'll be all right, mate. I promise."

#

Maeko woke with a start. The first thing she noticed, after the pain, was that Macak wasn't there. Fresh pain of a different kind twisted in her chest. She squeezed her eyes shut against the pain and began to sit up.

Someone touched her shoulder.

"You should not move yet. You will pull the stitches."

"Mum?" She opened her eyes.

Tomoe's smile was strained. She reached up a gentle hand and unnecessarily brushed Maeko's hair from her face.

Maeko lay back again, realizing from the pain in her side that her mother was right. She rested there and looked around. She was back in the room she and Tomoe shared at Drake's manor.

"Where's—"

"Chaff is down having some repairs done to his arm. I stitched and bandaged his head wound myself. He will be fine."

"That's wonderful, but—"

"Ash is down in the hanger studying the

metalsmithing technique of Drake's master smith. His shoulder injury will keep him from doing much work for a while, but he is well."

Frustration burst like a large bubble in her chest. "Macak! Where's Macak?"

Tomoe smiled gently and placed a hand on her arm. "I did what I could for him."

Panic sparked in Maeko. He'd been alive. Weak and injured, but alive. He couldn't have…

"They are fixing his leg downstairs now."

Maeko released a heavy exhale. "Mum. You scared me. I thought he was holding up a stone."

Tomoe looked puzzled. "Chaff?"

"Macak. Chaff and Ash were at least still standing on their own when we got to the airship."

"Oh." Tomoe lifted her shoulders in a tiny shrug.

She didn't appear to quite understand the bond between Maeko and Macak. There didn't seem much point in trying to explain it now.

"Macak will be well. Both Ash and Chaff are bruised and not quite as handsome as normal."

Maeko smirked. "You think they're handsome."

Tomoe nodded. "In very different ways. You would have lovely children with either."

She flushed. "Mum!"

Tomoe smiled to herself and stood. "You should rest more."

Maeko didn't think she could rest more, but sometime later she was awoken by a knock on the door. Her side still hurt like the dickens. Despite it, she managed to prop herself upright against some pillows before calling for her visitor to enter.

Drake stepped in through the door. He had some healing scratches on one cheek, but appeared otherwise unharmed.

"Good to see you awake."

"Good to see you didn't go down with your ship."

A grimace twisted his wolfish features for a few seconds. He approached the dresser near the bed and rested his hands on it, gazing out the window.

"If you three hadn't stopped that machine of theirs, we would have lost a lot more than my battleship. The parachutes your mother helped put together worked perfectly, even if the ship itself was short-lived."

Tomoe had sewn parachutes? She hid her surprise. "What happens now?"

"We got the queen's attention with this disaster. She's no longer supporting the Literati as an organization. They are officially disbanded and all their activities are to be stopped by royal decree. The Pirates have also been warned against organizing in any official manner. The Bobbies are being put back in charge of law enforcement in London. Thaddeus has been imprisoned and is being investigated in the death of his brother among other things. You took care of sentencing Joel."

She winced inwardly at that. No matter how she hated him, she didn't feel good about killing someone. "What about Bennett?"

Drake shrugged. "Vanished like a ghost."

Not a surprise.

"Were there any survivors found in the rubble?"

He shook his head. "Not that I know of."

Her chest tightened. She had condemned Travis to

death. Some wounds would never be healed and some wrongs couldn't be righted. She would have to live with that.

"I don't know who's name your guilt bears, but I can give you a long list of names of people who would probably be dead now if you hadn't been there."

"Thank you." It didn't make her feel better right now. In time, maybe. Maeko took a careful deep breath. "What about us?"

He looked at her now, meeting her gaze.

"I've offered Ash and Chaff both work here. Honest work," he added when she narrowed her eyes. "Ash is planning to go back to working with his father when his arm is healed, though he said he might consider later if the offer remains open. I could find work for you as well. We found the blueprints you saved in a briefcase buried under the rubble of a wall. There were also some other very incriminating documents in there that should help in the case against Thaddeus and the Lits. I think you got lucky quite a few times down there. I could use that kind of luck and skill, on my team. That said, Amos also expressed interest in offering you some kind of working arrangement. He said you would make a fine detective."

She smiled slightly at that. Could they do it? Could she and Amos start up where Em had left off? Maybe Chaff would be interested in working with them?

"Did Chaff accept your offer?"

Drake chuckled. "He said he wanted to talk to you first."

There was another knock on the door and Drake smiled.

"Right on time." He turned and started walking toward the door.

"Dominic," she called and he stopped in his tracks. "You helped found the Literati, didn't you?"

He glanced back at her. "It was never meant to become the monstrosity they made it into."

"What will you do with the blueprints?"

"I've got some contacts in Japan interested in the prosthesis work. For medical purposes," he added when she started to frown.

Leaving it at that, he walked over to the door and left as Chaff and Ash entered.

Her heart soared when she saw them, both with swollen, bruised faces, Ash's arm strapped up and Chaff bearing a large bandage around his head. In Chaff's arms rested a cleaned up black and white cat with a gleaming new clockwork leg. He carried the cat over and set him on the bed.

Macak walked over to her, moving a little slow, but very much alive. He climbed onto her lap and leaned against her chest, his eyes squinting closed with contentment when he looked up at her and began to purr. With one hand, she stroked the cat's head. With the other, she took Chaff's hand and smiled up at him and Ash. No matter what happened next, they were all alive and together right now and she couldn't imagine asking for more.

CHAPTER THIRTY

I t was raining. A light misting rain that could somehow make you wet faster than a heavy deluge. She could almost blame that rain for the moisture streaming down her cheeks, if not for the fancy umbrella Drake had loaned her that kept the rain away.

Amos stepped up to the grave, his feet squishing in the saturated grass. He set Em's hat by the gravestone then stepped back, folding his hands in front of him. The gesture was dignified. Respectful. Maeko didn't have much to offer, other than her tears. Those were steady and sincere. Em had been a mentor and, in some peculiar way, a parental figure at times. Em deserved better than this.

"Do you want to try it?" Amos's voice was soft, barely breaking through the sound of the rain misting down.

"I think I need a little more time to heal," she answered, even now feeling the pain in her side every time she breathed too deep. Macak butted his head into her cheek, reminding her that he was there and in need of affection. She smiled and scratched his head, her tears subsiding. "I'll contact you in a couple weeks and let you know. Drake offered to let me stay at the manor until I'm better."

And I can try to figure out more about what he's going to do with those blueprints before I go.

Amos nodded. "I'll look forward to hearing from you. For now, I've another grave to visit." He tipped his hat and walked away, going off to visit Rueben's grave now.

Ash and Chaff moved up alongside her. Chaff slid his hand into hers, fingers twining. Ash's face was still a little swollen and bruised from the broken nose. Chaff's head was also a bit bruised and swollen, but both were starting to look better.

"She was a remarkable woman," Maeko said.

Chaff squeezed her hand.

"So are you," Ash stated.

Maeko shifted her feet, uncomfortable with the praise.

"I think Em saw that. That's why she tried to apprentice you," Chaff remarked.

Ash gave her a sideways glance. "Are you going to try and follow in her footsteps?"

"I don't know. I mean, she had so much experience and she had two brilliant blokes to help her solve everything. Where would I find two good gentlemen like that?" She smirked.

"I'd tickle you silly for that if you weren't injured," Chaff said.

"Same here," Ash agreed.

Maeko grinned and pressed her cheek to Macak's head. "I have a feeling my side is going to hurt for a really long time."

Both of them chuckled. They turned with her and flanked her back to Drake's coach. Maybe she would try the detective thing. Maybe not. Maybe she could even talk Chaff or Ash, or perhaps both, into helping her with it. There was time to consider it while they all healed. For now, in this moment, she couldn't imagine wanting more than the four of them together without someone trying to kill any of them. That was good enough.

THE END

ACKNOWLEDGEMENTS

As always, there are many people in my life I'm leaving out here for brevity sake. All of you are still very important to me and I am always thankful for you.

To my mom Linda for your loving support and for helping me work out and refine my ideas.

To Rick and Ann for being two of the best of friends anyone could ask for and for being willing give honest feedback on my books.

To Aradia for knowing I would succeed from the first time we met and being an inspiration in your dedication to your own art.

To my cover artist, Mark, my editor M Evan, and my interior designer, Brian, thank you for your fantastic work and for being such amazing people to work with.

To my fans, for being awesome people and for pushing me to finish this book.

To my sixth-grade teacher, Mr. Johnson, for being so pleased and excited when I told you I was going to be an author and to my eighth-grade algebra teacher, Mr. Siebenlist, for almost letting me flunk because you were so delighted that I was writing books in class rather than notes.

AUTHOR BIO

Nikki started writing her first novel at the age of 12, which she still has tucked in a briefcase in her home office. She now lives in the magnificent Pacific Northwest tending to her sweet old horse and a wondrous cat-god. She feeds her imagination by sitting on the ocean in her kayak gazing out across the never-ending water or hanging from a rope in a cave, embraced by darkness and the sound of dripping water. She finds peace through practicing iaido or shooting her longbow.

•

Thank you for taking time to read this novel. Please leave a review if you enjoyed it.

•

For more about me and my work visit me at
http://elysiumpalace.com.

•

OTHER NOVELS by NIKKI McCORMACK

Made in the USA
Coppell, TX
07 January 2021